AMERICAN HOMICIDE DETECTIVE:

A GIFTED DETECTIVE PURSUES A SERIAL KILLER

CHARLES JASON SMITH

Print ISBN ....

Electronic ISBN .....

This book is a work of fiction. Names, characters, places, and events herein are either the product of the author's imagination or are used fictitiously. Any resemblance to actual persons, living or dead, is entirely coincidental.

❀ Created with Vellum

FOREWARD BY DETECTIVE TOM ARMELLI

Some of you may have heard of me or watched me as a Cleveland Homicide Detective on A&E Show *The First 48* and *Crime Show 360*. I met Charles years ago when we both started our careers as beat cops in the same police department.

We often ran into each other at the Justice Center in Cleveland, where all major criminal trials are held. We mostly knew each other by reputation. Charles was a hardworking, skilled, and honest cop. You never heard him brag about his high-profile arrests; in fact, when another officer asked him about an arrest, he would always respond, "It was a team effort."

Charles was promoted to sergeant, and later on became the team leader for the department's Warrant Fugitive Task force. He served the last seven years of his career in that role. During that time, he made many arrests including:

- A murder suspect who killed 3 people in Detroit and fled to Cleveland.
- A murder suspect who shot and killed a mother and two-year-old child in Jasper Alabama and fled to Cleveland.

Then, in the early 90s, there was a rash of violent home invasions, and in one instance, a local reporter rode with Charles to do a story on Channel 3 News. Charles' only request was not to show his face.

That same night, a 911 call came in from a mother who was alone with her child when a stranger broke in. The 911 call was chilling to listen to as the caller described hearing the suspect rifling through the kitchen drawer. It sounded as if he was getting a knife.

The suspect had kicked in a small panel in the entrance door to gain entry.

Charles was on the scene quickly and advised dispatch he was kicking down the door. Charles caught the suspect and arrested him just a few feet from the room where the victims were hiding.

This is the type of cop society needs.

Charles spent a great deal of time in The Cleveland Homicide Unit doing extensive research because he wanted his book to be 100% accurate. When he gave me a copy of the manuscript to read, I was amazed at what a gifted writer he was. I can guarantee you this will be one of the most amazing books you will ever read. Unlike other writers who simply research, then write a book, Charles is a real-life decorated cop who has experienced the life for real.

Det. Tom Armelli, Cleveland Police Homicide Unit, who has been featured on the first 48 and Crime 360.

DETECTIVE RALPH FRIEDMAN

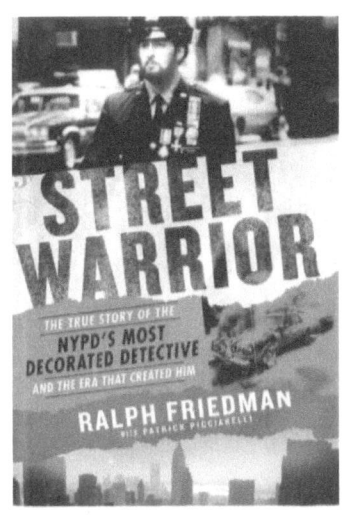

"American Homicide Detective" is one of the most compelling police thrillers you will ever read. It is an absolute page-turner that you can't put down. Charles is a gifted writer whose knowledge comes from being a police officer himself. His style of writing and crisp descriptions of the story line and characters will keep you wanting to know what's next . . .

Ret. NYPD Det. Ralph Friedman, co-author of the book "Street Warrior"
and star and subject of the TV series
"Street Justice-The Bronx."

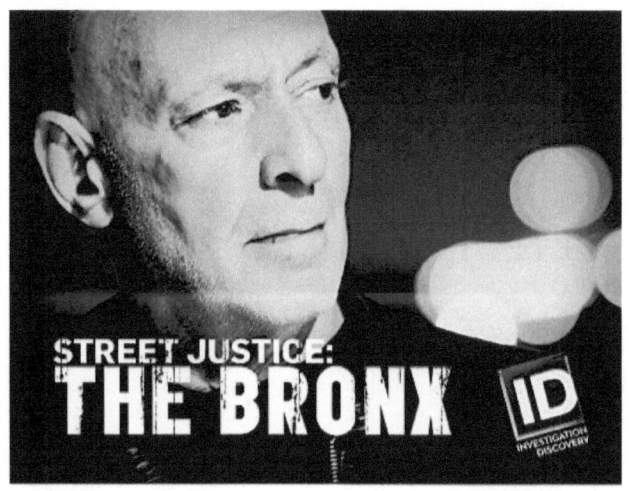

LT. RANDY SUTTON

"American Homicide Detective" provides the reader with a glimpse into a world rarely seen, the heart and soul of a cop. But this story is far from most in this genre. It takes topics of today and binds them around a gritty personal history of a cop bent on justice. Charles draws the reader in with his storytelling skills, and leaves you anxious to turn the next page until it slams you into the wall at the end. It's truly a great read."

Lt. Randy Sutton, retired from the Las Vegas Metro Police, is the Author of "A Cop's Life," Founder of "The Wounded Blue," and Host of "Blue Lives Radio"

www.thewoundedblue.org

TONY MINGO

I have known Charles for 20 years. We met at a gym that was frequented by cops. I was a Personal Trainer at the gym, and I became friends with him. Charles was a dedicated cop that kept himself in top physical shape. Around 2003, he released a book "Cop to CEO" which sold very well.

I left the gym to open my own business "Live Bettter Fit," and later, I heard Charles was injured in the line of duty. Charles contacted me and said, while on duty, he broke his neck and his back.

He was forced to retire from the police department due to his injuries. After several surgeries and physical therapy, Charles came to my new business to have me train him back to health. He was in a great deal of pain. At times, so bad I had to help him stand up from the floor.

Despite his condition, and it was bad, Charles continued to train. "I don't give up," he said.

Charles continued to train, and to my amazement, made dramatic improvements. During our time together, we became not only great friends but brothers.

Charles began to tell me about a goal he had to write a not only a novel but also a screenplay based on the book. Both were completed, and the title became "American Homicide Detective."

I am telling you he is a very gifted writer and his book is a must read.

Tony Mingo

www.livebetterfit.com

DAVE RANDALL

*C*harles provides a real-world account, yet fictional, of the life of a homicide detective. His detailed accounts seem almost like a non-fiction narrative because of his career as real-world beat police officer.

The book provides a chronological account of a fictional Cleveland homicide detective that importantly places each time period in a proper, and I argue, unique perspective. By weaving the narrative with a timeline of contemporary events and setting, he provides a rich account of what his characters are experiencing and dealing with as society changes. A very worthy effort and read that will delight any reader interested in this genre of pulp fiction.

David Randall, Ph.D.

Executive Director and Resident Scholar, American Research and Policy Institute.

GIACOMO GIAMMATTEO

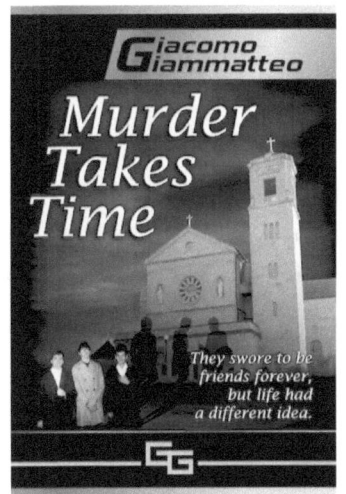

American Homicide Detective grabs your interest from the first few chapters and doesn't let go until the last page. Many books have slow spots in the middle; this one doesn't. It pulls you in deeper. Just when you think there is an opportunity to set the book down and catch some sleep, something happens to make you want to read more.

The thing I enjoyed most about the book was the credibility. I don't like reading books, where things are stated erroneously. That isn't the case here. A few times, I checked on a fact or statement made, and in each case, they proved to be true. After a while, it comes to be a comfortable feeling to know that you're dealing with someone who understands what they're talking about, and Smith is just that guy.

He's a long-time law-enforcement person who not only knows the business, but lived it.

I highly recommend the book.

Giacomo Giammatteo, author of many mystery books.

INTRODUCTION

What happens when a racist, bigoted, degenerate family marries into a good, caring family? Read *American Homicide Detective* and find out.

Johnny McCoy was raised by a loving, caring mother and a racist, bigoted father. His father hated anyone who wasn't lily white, and he beat those thoughts into Johnny every chance he got—both mentally and physically. At ten years old, Johnny learned to shoot like a marksman. At eleven, his father killed his mother, then himself.

Johnny fell in love with his friend's cousin at seventeen—a black girl named Liz. Then he joined the Marines to make something of himself. While he was away, a serial killer preying on young African-American women killed his love, and Johnny vowed to get even.

He got accepted into sniper school, and when he got out, he joined the police force, intent on stopping the lunacy that was still going on.

TIME TO DO SOMETHING

SPRING 2001, CLEVELAND, OHIO

Johnny lay in bed, wide awake. He needed sleep, and he *wanted* to sleep, but he couldn't sleep no matter how he tried.

Tony and Ronnie were already asleep; he could hear them rolling over in bed, not to mention being kicked a few times by Ronnie, who was a restless sleeper.

He also heard the noise the cars made as they went up and down the street in front of the house. He heard the neighborhood dogs barking continually—the ones who were left outside—and worst of all, he heard Uncle Dominic and Aunt Clorinda arguing about money that was spent and worrying over where they'd get enough to pay the bills and feed the kids both.

He hated to hear them argue, but at least it helped him make up his mind. He was going to enlist. He hadn't decided yet if it would be Marines or Army, but he had narrowed it down to those two. He thought about what he knew of each one, and he wondered which one he should choose. As he pondered on that, the noises that kept him awake faded, and he finally fell asleep.

Johnny woke early and jumped out of bed, eager to start the day. It would be the first day of his new life. A life where he intended to make a difference. He went to the bathroom, shaved, brushed his teeth, and took care of other business, then he bounded down the steps.

He wore a big smile as he entered the kitchen and greeted Aunt Clorinda and Uncle Dom. "Morning, guys. How's the day going?"

"Too damn easy to tell," Dominic said.

Johnny helped himself to a cup of the coffee that seemed to be always brewing at Uncle Dom's house, then joined them at the table.

"What's on your plate today?" Aunt Clorinda asked.

He finished chewing on a bite of bagel, then looked at both of them. "Not much, unless you count enlisting as something of interest."

"What? Enlisting where?" Dominic asked.

"The Marines," Johnny said. "I decided last night. All I need is written permission from you and a ride to the recruiting station from Brandon."

"Are you nuts?" Dominic asked. "People get killed doing that shit."

"Uncle Dom, hardly anyone gets killed; besides, there's no war going on. I'm joining for the training and to learn things."

"There may not be a war today, but give it a month or two. This damn country can't go long without picking a fight with somebody or sticking their nose where it doesn't belong."

Johnny laughed, but to himself so he didn't stir up his uncle. Once you got Dominic on a rant, it was difficult to stop him. And when he got like that, no other ideas were heard.

"You're a cop, Uncle Dom. Almost the same thing."

"Like hell. If you want to be a cop, wait a few years, and I'll make sure you get in. *If* you keep your nose clean, that is. If not, I'll lock your ass up."

Uncle Dominic always complained about the government doing this or that, but he'd served as a policeman for more than twenty years now, and he was a damn good one. He also continually threatened to lock Johnny up or something else, but the truth was, he'd do anything to help him. He just didn't like saying so.

"Come on, Uncle Dom. You know you want to see me come home in uniform, and don't try saying different."

He laughed. "All right, give me the damn papers, and I'll sign them. You sure about the age thing?"

Johnny nodded. "You've got to be eighteen to join on your own, but only seventeen if you have a parent or guardian's written permission."

Johnny opened a folder filled with papers and set the necessary ones in front of his uncle, who either read them quickly, or pretended to, then signed.

"All right, as soon as the ink dries, you'll have your permission. But don't try sneaking off without giving Aunt Clorinda a big kiss goodbye. And you know she's gonna want to fix you a huge send-off meal."

"And I'll be happy to eat it," Johnny said, then he stood and hugged his aunt. "You know I'm gonna miss you, Aunt Clorinda."

"You sure as hell better," she said, and dabbed at a few tears with a tissue she always had stuffed in her apron pocket.

Johnny put his dishes in the sink, then left and started up the steps.

15

"And don't forget to say goodbye to your brothers," Aunt Clorinda hollered.

"I won't, Aunt Clorinda, you know that. In fact, I'm going up to wake them right now."

Tony and Ronnie weren't really Johnny's brothers; in fact, Ronnie wasn't even Ronnie's name. His real name was Rinaldo, named after Uncle Dom's grandfather. They weren't brothers, but they were family; they were cousins, and Johnny had been raised the past six years alongside them as if they were brothers. As far as he was concerned, they *were* brothers. As much as anybody was, they were.

Johnny sneaked into the room, being as quiet as he could. When he got near the bed, he tossed a few drops of water on their faces and hollered, "Time to get up, lazy asses."

Tony and Ronnie jumped from bed, both of them cursing. "You son of a bitch! You damn son of a bitch."

Johnny laughed and sat on the edge of the bed. "Sorry to wake you guys, but I wanted to tell you that I'm leaving today."

"Leaving where?" Ronnie asked.

"Where are you going?" Tony asked.

"Joining the Marines," he said.

"The Marines? No shit?"

"Yeah, Tony. No shit."

"Man, that's cool," Ronnie said. "I wish I could go with you."

"They wouldn't take you even if Uncle Dom would allow it. You've got to be seventeen *with* permission and eighteen without it."

"You lucky bitch," Tony said. "Where you think they'll send you?"

Johnny shook his head. "No idea yet. Have to wait until I get in, I guess."

"Who's taking you down?" Ronnie asked. "Is Dad driving you?"

"No, Brandon's coming over to pick me up. I called a little while ago."

"You better write," Tony said. "And send postcards with pictures of where you go."

"I doubt it will be anywhere nice," Johnny said. "But I'll do it just to shut you up."

The beeping of a horn stopped the conversation. Johnny pulled the sheet that was draped over the window aside and looked out. "It's Brandon," he said. "Gotta go. See you guys later."

Johnny bounded down the stairs and out the front door, then hopped into the front seat next to Brandon. "Thanks for coming B. I appreciate it."

"Where we off to?"

"Maple Heights," Johnny said. "I'm signing up today."

"What? For real? The Marines?"

Johnny nodded. "The damn Marines, B. I'm gonna be a Marine."

BASIC TRAINING

SPRING 2001

Johnny entered the recruiting office feeling a little nervous. He was a big kid, big even for a full-grown man, but he'd heard tales about what the training was like, and it wasn't for pussies. The worst thing he could imagine was being kicked out—if they did that stuff.

The only good thing was that it was 2001, and the world was at peace—relative peace. Iran wasn't causing any trouble—not now—and while there were rumblings of discontent elsewhere in the Middle East, nothing had happened yet. That meant the US wasn't involved in any ongoing wars.

But it won't be long before we are.

Johnny waited in line behind two men who looked to be in their twenties. After a short while, he stood before the recruiter and handed him the signed papers from his Uncle Dom, and his license and birth certificate. He stood rigid. "Need anything else, sir?"

"First, I'm not a 'sir,' so don't call me one. Do that when you're in service, and the DI will kick your ass. DIs are called DI, drill sergeant, or just sergeant, but they don't like to be called 'sir.' Now wait while I process this. It won't take long."

A half an hour later, the recruiter sat back and sighed. "There, done with that."

Johnny felt relieved, and he smiled broadly to show it. "So I'm a Marine now?"

The recruiter laughed. "Not hardly, son. You're far from it."

He handed Johnny a card with his name written on it. "Take a few steps back and hold this in front of you. Stand still while I take your photo."

Johnny held the card chest-high and stood as tall as rigid as he could.

"Okay, good," the recruiter said, and handed Johnny some papers. "Now find your ass a place to sit and take this test. This will tell us where we should put you when you get to boot camp. You'll be lucky if they take you at all."

Johnny started to walk away, and the recruiter hollered. "You'll leave when I say so, boy."

Johnny spun around and once again stood at attention.

"All right," the recruiter said. "And while you fill out those answers, keep asking yourself why the hell you want to do this. When you finish, report back here and we'll determine if you're qualified for anything other than taking up space."

"And if I am qualified? What then?"

The recruiter laughed, and it seemed cynical. "If you qualify, you can count your blessings or curse your fate. We've got a bus leaving for Parris Island tonight at seven. If you're five minutes late, start running in the other direction because the bus will be gone, and I'll be after your ass." He stared at Johnny. "Got that?"

"Yes, corporal," Johnny said.

The recruiter smiled. "Well, you're starting off all right. Now get away from me and do like I said."

Johnny snapped a salute and made his way to the table, where he completed the papers the corporal had given him. He handed the papers to the corporal and asked, "What now?"

"You can wait in a chair, take a ride, or shit in your hat, but whatever you do, be back here by 0600—that's zero six hundred—to hear your assignment and get your papers."

Brandon was waiting in the car, listening to the radio, when Johnny got in. "Well?"

"I'm not a Marine yet, but I'm on my way," Johnny said. "I'm supposed to report back at six."

"Hot dog," Brandon said. "A damn Marine."

"I just hope I can make it."

"What the hell are you worried about? You're the fittest guy I know."

"I know, but being fit for high school and fit for the Marines are different things."

"Can't be that much different," Brandon said. "You'll do fine. By the way, where you going for training?"

"Parris Island," Johnny said. "Assuming I make it."

"Parris Island? Where's that, in France?"

Johnny laughed. "No, dumb ass. It's in South Carolina."

"Shit, that's pretty close to Florida. Bet they have some hot chics down there."

~

Johnny reported back to the recruiting station at six that day. He was told he was accepted, and, based on his answers, he was recommended for MOS 0311, which is an infantry rifleman. That excited him as much as being accepted. After silently rejoicing, he boarded the bus bound for Parris Island.

It was a boring ride, and his nerves made it seem even longer than the fourteen hours it took. Fortunately, it was almost all interstate, so delays were minimal.

When they got off the bus, they were immediately set upon by several DIs (drill instructors) who seemed to do nothing but yell.

By the end of week two, he had been through hell several times, and he wondered if it would ever end. Half a dozen guys had already washed out and were sent home. Johnny made up his mind right then that nothing would make him give up. *Nothing.*

Week three rolled around and Monday morning seemed to start the same. DI Benz was, once again, ahead of the sun as he burst through the doors. "All I see is a barracks filled with lazy asses. All right, we're gonna fix that. From now on, the last one dressed and ready has to run three miles, followed by one hundred pushups. Got that?"

"Yes, Sergeant," everyone yelled.

"We're gonna do things differently today," DI Benz said. "Grab the rifles you were assigned and follow me."

Johnny's heart beat faster, so fast he was afraid it could be heard. He'd been waiting for this since he got here. He might finally be able to show his stuff.

They marched to a large field with a line of sand bags along the side of the trail. In the field to the south, about fifty yards out, sat a row of targets.

"Get your asses down and rest your guns on the sandbags. When I call your name, and *only* when I call your name, you are to take three shots at the target directly in front of you. Is that understood?"

"Yes, Sergeant," everyone yelled again.

"Good, then let's start. Johnson," Benz yelled.

Flick Johnson was first in line. When Benz called his name, he lay down, lined up his gun, took aim, and fired three times.

Benz called a stop and told everyone to lay their guns down. He then radioed the spotters, who were safely behind a bank of sand behind the targets. They checked Flick's target and called back. "One three inches right of center. Two complete misses."

Benz grinned. "Where'd you learn to shoot, Johnson?"

"My uncle."

"Tell your uncle he stinks as a teacher."

Benz took a few steps and called out another name. "Raston, you're up."

Raston took hold of his rifle, aimed, and fired three times.

Benz went through the same drill with the spotters.

"One four inches left of center. One two inches below center. And one miss."

"Raston, you and Johnson need to find another teacher," Benz said, then took two more steps. "McCoy."

Johnny took several deep breaths, picked up his rifle, and aimed at the target. His gut roiled, and his hands trembled.

What if I miss? What if I mess up?

He recalled the instructions he'd gotten when young, then he slowly squeezed the trigger three times.

Benz called the spotters, but there was a slight delay. "Anybody alive down there?" he asked.

"We were just verifying," the spotter said.

Benz laughed. "What? Miss all of them?"

"No, Sergeant. All three in the center."

"Check again," Benz said.

"We've already checked twice, sir. All three in the center, and one was dead center."

Benz knelt next to Johnny. "Let them change the target, then I want you to take three more shots."

"Yes, Sergeant," Johnny said.

A moment later, Benz gave the okay to fire.

Once again, Johnny took his time, breathed deeply, took aim, then fired.

The spotters called in a moment later. "Three more in the center. Two of them are dead center."

"Replace the target one more time, but save the originals."

Benz tapped Johnny with his boot. "When the new target is up, I want you to go again, but this time I want you to fire six shots, and don't take so long. Make it rapid-fire."

Johnny nodded.

A moment later, Benz said, "Okay, McCoy, it's ready."

Johnny took a deep breath, aimed, and rapidly fired six shots, then lay his rifle beside him.

Benz waited for the spotter to call. "Five in the center. One an inch to the right."

"Have those targets delivered to my admin immediately," Benz said. He looked down at Johnny and said, "Damn good shooting. Damn good."

Benz finished out the day, allowing all the men to shoot, but only one other person even got two in the center, and both of them barely made it. He took everyone back to the barracks and told them to clean up and have fun that night. Afterward, he made his way to the lieutenant's office after picking up the targets.

He knocked on the door and went in when invited. "What is it, sergeant?"

"Sir, I wanted to show you the results of our shooting practice." He laid the three targets on the desk and stepped back.

The lieutenant examined them and nodded. "This was the standard fifty yards?"

"Yes, sir," Benz said.

"Seems as if you have a couple of sharpshooters in your outfit, Benz."

"No, sir. Just one. One man did all three of those. Eleven of twelve shots in the center."

"Nonsense," the lieutenant said, and picked up the targets to look again. "You're telling me that one man shot all of these?"

"Yes, sir. His name's McCoy, sir."

"How many tries did he have to get this?"

"Just the three, sir. Those were his only three attempts."

"I find it hard to believe, Sergeant. I've never seen shooting like this. Maybe Bentley, but only near the end of his training."

"I agree, sir. I think we need to explore this. He should be pushed toward sniper school if everything else checks out. You know we never have enough snipers."

The lieutenant stared. "Where's Bentley now? Do you know?"

"I believe he's at Camp Lejeune, sir. At least, the last I heard, he was."

"Sergeant, send an inquiry. If he's still there, see if he can get here by Friday. I'd like to see this McCoy go up against real competition."

"Will do, sir. Right away." Benz reached for the targets, but the lieutenant held onto them. "Leave these. I want to show them to the captain."

Benz snapped a salute and exited. He showered and changed clothes, then joined the men at the local pub, something he wouldn't ordinarily do.

Johnny sat at the end of the bar, slugging shots as if it were party night. Benz approached and tapped him on the shoulder. "McCoy, none of my business, but you might want to take it easy on the booze. I suspect we'll have at least one visitor wearing stripes tomorrow and maybe more."

Johnny set a half-full shot glass on the bar. "You mean the lieutenant?"

"At least the lieutenant and maybe the captain. I showed him your targets, and he was impressed. He even mentioned getting a former crack shot back here to check you out. I don't know if he will, but that's the direction he's thinking."

Johnny pushed the glass aside, then took the bottle in front of him and slid it down the bar. "You guys finish this up, but don't forget you owe me one." He then got up and walked out of the pub.

Benz watched him leave and smiled. *The kid might be all right.*

LET'S SEE HIM SHOOT

PARRIS ISLAND, SOUTH CAROLINA
—BOOT CAMP

Johnny didn't sleep well that night. Most of the time he spent worrying about his performance and what it would be like if the lieutenant showed up to see him shoot.

In the morning, he was even more nervous, and by the time he got to the shooting range, he felt like he did when he was a kid, back when he went to the range with his dad. And that's something he *never* wanted to feel again.

By day's end, the lieutenant hadn't shown though, and neither had anyone else. In hindsight, it was a shame because Johnny's shooting mirrored what he'd done the day before. If anything, it might have been a hair better.

He received multiple pats on the back during the return to the barracks, and he got several invitations to meet at the pub for a beer or a shot.

As much as he wanted to, he declined, opting to stay at the barracks, preparing his mind for the next day. If he kept shooting like this, he knew top brass would come soon. He wanted to be ready.

For final preparation, he reviewed everything he'd been taught. For as much of an asshole as his father was, he did give good advice regarding how to shoot, and it would be a shame to let that go to waste.

His father's loud, harsh voice rang in his ears. He pictured him hovering above, pointing his meaty fingers and yelling.

Yelling. It was always yelling. Never teaching or advising.

"If you're gonna learn to shoot right—and you will—you need to know the basics," he said. "First is . . ."

Johnny pulled out a folded-up paper he kept in his breast pocket. It was creased so badly it looked as if it would fall apart.

He slowly opened it and read:

1. Mechanical — make sure everything is working smoothly —the scope, the trigger, all parts are oiled, the grip is tight and firm, etc.
2. Ammunition — test out different loads until you find one or two you're happy with, then try to stick to that.
3. Clean — Clean, clean, clean. Clean your rifle tip to grip. Scrub that barrel clean. Make sure your receiver is clean as well and that all parts are lubricated. If your rifle is fed with detachable magazines, make sure they're clean and working well too.
4. Get fit — Breathing right and dealing with stress are as much a part of shooting as the trigger pull and keeping your equipment in top shape.
5. Learn how to breathe slowly and calm yourself before you

pull the trigger. If possible, take several deep breaths before each shot.

Johnny's father wasn't the best shot, but he was damn good. And he had a lot of good advice, even if it was offered in a bad manner.

There was a time—long ago—when Johnny had those rules memorized and could recite them when asked. During recent years, he had let the memories slip, but they came flooding back. Johnny read the 'rules' over and over until he once again had them committed to memory. Before the week was up, he'd need them.

On Thursday, Bentley showed up at the lieutenant's office. He saluted, then said, "I was told you requested me to come here, sir."

The lieutenant smiled and extended his hand. "At ease. Good to see you again, Bentley. It's been a while."

"Yes, sir. It has."

"Let me get right to the point."

"Please do, sir."

"The reason I asked you here is to evaluate, and help if you see fit, a recruit we have."

"Sir?"

"He's only been here three weeks, and he . . ." The lieutenant stood and opened the file cabinet. "It is probably best to show you." He pulled out the targets McCoy had shot and handed them to Bentley.

Bentley stared at each one for a few seconds before moving on to the next one. "And you say this kid's a recruit?"

"Got here three weeks ago."

"If he holds up, I'd venture to say you got yourself a world-class sniper in the making. Mind you, there's a lot more to being a sniper than just shooting, but shooting is priority one, and the kid definitely has that."

"Would you be willing to watch him tomorrow morning?"

"I'd be happy to."

"Good, we'll leave here at six."

Bentley stood and shook hands. "See you then, sir."

By the time the lieutenant and Bentley arrived, several of the men had already shot, but Benz had held back on McCoy, knowing who was coming.

"Attention," Benz yelled.

All the men stood and saluted. "Men, we have with us today, one of the best, if *not* the best. He rose in rank from marksman, to sharp-shooter, to expert in less time than anyone we had before."

"You ain't seen McCoy shoot, lieutenant."

The lieutenant smiled. "I know I haven't. Not yet, but that's what I'm here for."

Benz gestured to his left, and the lieutenant walked over to Johnny. "Marine, I'm told you can shoot."

"Yes, sir. I hope it's satisfactory, sir."

"All right, let's see if it is. That's why Bentley is here today—to judge your skills. So why don't you get in position and show us what you can do."

Johnny snapped a salute and lay down with his rifle next to him. "Ready, sir."

Benz radioed the spotters, who raised a flag, indicating they were ready. Johnny breathed deeply and exhaled slowly several times, then he took aim and fired. He continued for six shots until Benz ordered him to stop.

The spotters verified the target, then called it in. "Six in the center. Three dead center."

Bentley nodded. "Damn good, Marine. Let's see a round of twelve, and do it rapid-fire if you will." He turned to Benz and said, "And have them move the targets back fifty yards."

Two minutes later, they signaled the targets were ready. "Have at it, McCoy," Benz said.

"Will do," Johnny said. He repeated his process of breathing, then aiming and shooting. This time he fired rapidly, firing twelve shots in less time than it took him to fire six.

A moment later, the spotters radioed in. "Ten center. One a near miss on the left. And one a miss by two inches on the right."

"Son of a bitch," Bentley said. "Can you retrieve that target for me? I want to see it."

Benz had both targets brought up and handed them to Bentley. He examined them closely, then went to McCoy. "Do you know how good this is?"

"Not by comparison. No."

"Well, I can tell you it is better than what I did when I *left* here, and at three weeks in, I wasn't near this good."

Inside, Johnny smiled. Hell, he almost laughed. He'd done it, and he hadn't choked. "Thank you."

"One more test," Bentley said. "Actually two more. I'd like you to show me a spread of six from a kneeling position and a spread of six from a standing position. And I'm pushing the targets back another hundred yards. This will seem far—and it is—but with shooting like yours, you should be fine."

"I can do that," Johnny said, and assumed a kneeling position.

Once the targets were moved, Benz said, "Anytime you're ready."

Johnny breathed, aimed, and fired—six rapid shots. They changed targets, then he stood and did the same. When he was done, the spotters verified the targets and called in.

"Kneeling position shows four center. One near miss to the upper right, and one miss to the lower left."

"And the standing?" Benz asked.

"Standing is . . . Wait, Sergeant. Let me verify this." The spotter came back on in a few seconds. "Standing is six center. Two dead center."

Bentley laughed and slapped Johnny on the back. "Hot damn. You ready to go out and shoot some people?"

"I don't know. I guess, but who will I be shooting?"

"That don't hardly matter. You shoot whoever the hell they tell you to. One thing's for sure—I wouldn't want to be any of the ones they point you at."

Johnny lowered his head in embarrassment. He wasn't used to praise like this, only hollering.

"Thank you. I'll try."

"The hell with trying. From what I've seen, you're done trying. You're *doing*."

Bentley then looked to the lieutenant. "With your permission, sir. I'd like to take them all over to the pub. I think they deserve a reward."

"Permission granted, Bentley. And thank you."

Twelve thirsty Marines met Bentley at the pub, all eager to have a good time. Johnny sat next to Bentley.

"You're a sniper?"

Bentley nodded. "I am. Haven't done much sniping, but I try to stay prepared. There's a lot more to being a sniper than just shooting. You'll learn that though."

"I don't know if that's the route I want to go, but I *am* thinking about it."

Bentley looked over, eyebrows raised. "Why the hell not? You're the best damn shot I've seen. You'd make an excellent one."

Johnny cocked his head to one side. "I don't know. It's just . . ."

"Just what? Don't know if you want to kill people?"

"Kind of. It's not the killing. At least, I don't think it is. It's more the killing someone who's not expecting it. What I'm trying to say is if I was in a firefight, it would be easy, or at least easier, to shoot someone. But to hide behind a tree or on a rooftop and just shoot someone . . . I don't know."

"I hear you. I dealt with that too. But once you realize you're doing it for your country and to protect your fellow Marines or other soldiers, I think your reluctance will go away."

"I hope so," Johnny said. "I really hope so."

Bentley sipped on a beer, then looked over to Johnny. "Let me ask you something. Where the hell did you learn to shoot like that?"

Johnny felt shame and embarrassment. He didn't *want* to answer Bentley's question, but at the same time, he *did* want to. He wanted to tell anyone who would listen to what an ass his father had been, and what he'd done to his family.

He thought about what to say and decided to play it smart. After all, he didn't want to tell the truth and have some damn shrink bothering him every week. "A family member taught me," he said. Nothing more.

THE SHOOTING RANGE

SEVEN YEARS EARLIER (1994)—CLEVELAND, OHIO

Michael McCoy finished tying the shoelaces of his steel-tipped workbooks, buttoned his shirt, then headed for the door. "Time to go, little shit. Come on, hurry it up."

Johnny rushed to finish his cereal, grabbed his hat, and ran after his dad. He didn't want to risk being late. Not today. Today was shooting-range day, and that was as sacred as Christmas to his father.

The range was a five-mile drive from the house, and it may have been the only time Johnny remembered his father being happy—during that drive.

A few moments later, they pulled into the parking lot, filled with mud-splattered pickup trucks that were plastered with hunting stickers and many that sported gun racks behind the seat.

As they walked to the entrance, Michael slapped Johnny on the back. "You're gonna do good today, boy. I want you to show them what a man you are."

Johnny nodded. "I will," he said.

His father got him set up to shoot, using a Remington M24. He preferred the Barrett M82, but they didn't have one here to use. But that was all right. The M24 had been good for decades; it would do now.

Two or three of Michael's acquaintances gathered around, waiting for Johnny to shoot. A couple even took bets on whether he'd hit the bullseye.

Johnny trembled from nerves as he stepped up to take aim. He knew the consequences if he missed. He sighted down the scope, aimed, and fired.

"Son of a bitch," his father said. "Go again."

Once more, Johnny took aim and fired, but the result was the same —another miss.

Michael McCoy slapped his son on the side of the head, and not a playful slap either. It left a clear impression of his meaty hand. "You piece of crap. Can't you do anything right? I spent all that time teaching you to shoot, and you can't hit a thing. Wasted my goddamn time is what I did."

Johnny wiped away the tears streaming down his cheeks. He was only ten years old, but he could take a beating; he'd had plenty of experience doing that. The continual yelling was another thing. At times, Johnny felt it was worse than being hit. Besides, Johnny knew his aim was good. He was just off today. He couldn't say that to his father though. If he did, a beating would surely follow.

"What good are you, boy? You can't do shit." Johnny cowered and covered his head, expecting a beating like so many times before. His father was furious, and when he got like that, he normally resorted to violence. Johnny was often the receiving end of that violence, and he had the bruises and scars to show for it—even broken bones.

Johnny tried not to cry. "I'll do better, Dad. Promise."

"You goddamn better," his father said and raised his hand. He must have thought better of striking Johnny, because a moment later, Michael lowered his hand, mumbling as he did. "Worthless piece of shit."

Even though he wasn't told to, Johnny took aim and fired another round, but he missed the bullseye again. Michael pushed him out of the way, knocking him to the ground, then took his place behind the gun. "This is how it's done," he said, and fired two rounds into the target—both dead center. "When you learn to shoot like that, you'll be a man."

Johnny wanted to say something in response, but he held back. There was no sense in being smacked.

Michael glanced over at Johnny and must have seen the look on his face. "You say one word, boy, and I'll smack the shit out of you. Hear me?"

Johnny nodded.

Michael took a step toward him and hit him with the back of his hand, knocking Johnny to the ground. "When I ask you a question, I expect more than a nod of your head. Hear me?"

"Yes, sir," Johnny said as he picked himself up. "I hear you."

"That's good. You better listen or you're in for a world of hurt. I'm not gonna have you aim for some spic or nigger and miss. If you're gonna aim for something, you sure as shit better hit it."

Johnny wasn't going to say anything, but he felt as if he had to. "Dad, I don't want to shoot *anybody*. Why would I want to shoot somebody?"

"You don't want to eradicate those black specks of dirt we have amongst us? Huh?"

Johnny shook his head while cowering. "Why should I? They haven't done anything to me."

"You only *think* they haven't. They're ruining our society is what they're doing. Them and the chinks. Not a good person between them."

"That's not what my teacher says."

"Yeah, well, he's a bleeding-heart piece of shit who doesn't have to live in the world those people are busy ruining. If he did, he'd think different."

Michael picked up the rifle and headed toward the check-in desk. "Get moving, boy, or I'll leave your ass here."

Johnny rushed to catch up to his father, who had just opened the door. "Maybe I should do that anyway. Might teach you a goddamn lesson."

Johnny edged closer to his father. He didn't want to have to walk home. Not again.

YOUR FRIENDS ARE WHO I SAY THEY ARE

1995—CLEVELAND, OHIO

Johnny got up and ran down the stairs. He grabbed a piece of bread on his way out the door.

"Hey, young man, you've got to eat something, you know. You can't go all day without food."

"I know that, Mom, but I'm gonna be late if I don't hurry. Besides, I got some bread."

Sandy shook her head as the door banged shut. *That old screen door won't take much more.*

As Johnny raced across the front yard, he picked up his baseball bat, then jumped up and pulled an apple from a low-hanging branch. He bit into it as he ran toward the park. *Hope we got enough guys to play today.*

When Johnny arrived, there were only six kids at the ball field. "Where the hell is everybody?" Johnny asked. "Everybody knew we had a game."

"Maybe they're just late," Richie said. "Let's give it a few minutes."

The boys hung around playing catch and even doing batting practice, but after half an hour, no one showed. "Doesn't look good," Richie said.

Yelling and hollering from across the park drew Johnny's attention. A group of kids just walked onto the field. "Looks like they got almost enough for two full teams. If we joined up, we'd have enough."

"Yeah, but they're black," Ronnie said. "It doesn't bother me, but your dad might get pissed."

"What difference does it make?" Johnny asked. "Willie Mays was black."

"I say we go over," Richie said.

"Let's go," Johnny said, and everyone else joined in, picking up their gloves and bats and walking across the field. A couple of kids acted as if they wouldn't join them, but eventually they did.

When Johnny and the rest of them reached the field, he hollered out. "I'm Johnny McCoy. You guys need some players to fill out the team?"

The first baseman yelled, "Not no white boys. Hell no."

The pitcher walked over and extended his hand. "I'm Brandon. Pay no attention to that ass because, yeah, we do need some players. Get over by the dugout, and we'll start again and pick teams."

Johnny smiled and patted Brandon on the back. "Sounds good. I usually play shortstop, and Richie here is a catcher. The rest of them will play any position you need. I don't guarantee they'll be good, but they'll try."

Brandon laughed. "All we can ask for," he said. "Let's get started."

Choosing teams only took a few minutes, then they got started. In the bottom of the fourth inning, Johnny was up to bat and Brandon was pitching. He threw two strikes and one ball, then on the next pitch, it was near the outside corner. The umpire, a local coach who often refereed the games, called it a strike, which meant Johnny was out.

"No way," Johnny said. "No way that was a strike."

Brandon laughed. "You heard the ump, and you can't argue with an ump. You're out."

"Fuck you . . ." Johnny said.

Brandon tossed his glove in the dirt and rushed to home plate. Johnny met him halfway. "Nigger? Is that what you were gonna call me, you cracker son of a bitch? I'm gonna kick your ass."

"Go ahead and try," Johnny said, and swung the first punch, connecting with the side of Brandon's cheek.

Brandon hit back, then tackled Johnny to the ground, where they rolled in the dirt, punching each other. After a few minutes, the coach broke it up.

"All right, boys. Enough of this shit. If I have to put up with this, you can forget me umping forever."

"Sorry, Coach," Brandon said.

Johnny hesitated, but then said "Sorry."

"Forgetting something?" Coach asked.

Brandon turned around and held his hand out. "Sorry, Johnny. I lost my temper."

Shocked as he was, Johnny found the wherewithal to respond. "Me too, Brandon. And just so you know, I wasn't going to call you that. I wouldn't say that."

43

"Let's forget it, okay. I just want to win this game," Brandon said.

"If you learn how to pitch, I'll make sure you don't," Johnny said.

They both laughed and went back to their team, Brandon to the pitcher's mound and Johnny toward the dugout.

"Get back to bat," Brandon hollered. "I'm gonna strike you out fair and square. I don't want you saying you were cheated."

Johnny hesitated, then smiled. He walked back to the plate and assumed his stance. "Let's have it then."

An hour later, the game was over, and Brandon and his team had won. All the boys shook hands, then went their way. "How about next week?" Johnny hollered.

"If you like losing, be here about nine on Saturday."

"Count on us being here," Johnny said, and waved as he walked off.

Johnny tried sneaking into the house as quietly as possible, but his mother saw him from the kitchen. "Johnny, you're home. Come in and get something to eat. I just made soup."

"I'm good, Mom," he said, and started up the steps.

Just then, his father came around the corner. He reached out, grabbed a handful of Johnny's hair, and yanked him back.

"What the hell happened to you?" he asked.

"Nothing," Johnny said.

"Nothing, my ass. Look at your face. It's all scratched up." His father leaned closer. "And your eye, for Christ's sake. You got a black eye."

"It's nothing, Dad. I had to slide into second, and I collided with Richie."

"Bullshit!" his father said. "Those marks ain't from colliding into someone at second. You were in a fight and don't tell me you weren't."

"Okay. Okay, it was no big deal. I had an argument over a called strike."

"Who did you fight?"

"I don't know, some kid."

"What kid? I want to know."

"I don't know, Dad. He was a new kid."

"Black or white?"

"What?"

"Was the kid black or white? That's an easy question. Now answer me."

"Dad, what difference does it make? It was just two kids fighting over a call."

"So he was black, huh? A goddamn nigger. A god—"

"Dad . . ."

Michael smacked Johnny backhanded, knocking him to the floor. "Don't *ever* interrupt me, boy. *Never.*"

"Michael!" Sandy yelled as she ran in from the kitchen. "He's a boy, for God's sake."

"He's a boy who needs to learn manners," Michael said. He turned to Sandy and raised his hand. "And if you ever interrupt me, I'll smack the shit out of you, too. Don't think I won't."

Johnny grabbed hold of the railing and pulled himself up. "Mom, it's all right. I'm fine."

Sandy wrapped her arms around him and pulled him close. "You touch him again, and I'll see you pay for it," she said.

Michael sneered. "Oh, you will huh, bitch?"

Sandy gritted her teeth, leaned close to him and whispered, "Yeah, I will, Michael. I'll see you *die*. I'll *make sure* you die."

"Okay, guys. Enough fighting. I'm fine. I'm gonna wash up now, then later I'll be down for dinner."

As Johnny climbed the stairs, his father yelled, "Just remember who pays for the food you eat, you ungrateful shit."

Johnny gritted his teeth and clenched his jaw. He wanted to turn around and smack him, but that would be a death sentence; instead, he said, "I know, Dad, and I appreciate it," then continued his walk upstairs.

He stared in the mirror and scrubbed his face, wiping off the dirt and grimacing when the washcloth brushed over one of the scraped areas. All in all, it didn't look so bad though. A black eye and a few scrapes, but once he washed the dirt off, it wasn't much. *Don't know what the hell he was complaining about. I've gotten worse playing with Tony and Ronnie.*

Johnny was about to go downstairs, but decided to take a quick nap. He was tired from playing, so he went into his room and lay down.

A 'quick nap' turned into two hours, and he might not have woken then if it weren't for his mom calling him for supper.

"Johnny, time to get up, lazy head. It's almost dinner time, and I need the table set."

Johnny wiped the sleep from his eyes, drawing another grimace as his hands rubbed against the cuts and scrapes. "Coming, Mom. Only be a minute."

He rushed to the bathroom, washed his hands, then went downstairs.

He grabbed three plates and the accompanying silverware and placed them on the table.

"Did you wash your hands?" his mother asked. "I didn't see you do it."

Johnny sighed. "Yes, Mom. I washed them upstairs."

Sandy was still putting food on the table when Michael sat down. "Get me a beer, boy."

"I will," Johnny said. "I'm finishing up now."

"I didn't ask you what you were doing. I said, 'get me a beer,' and I don't expect excuses."

Johnny stopped what he was doing and walked to the fridge. "One or two?" he asked.

Michael shook his head. "I guess you don't learn in school either. I said get me a beer—*a* beer. I didn't say get me two beers. When I want another beer, I'll tell you."

Johny closed the fridge door and handed his father the beer. "Here you go," he said.

A few minutes into dinner, his father slapped his hand on the table, creating a loud noise. "I'm gonna say this now, boy. If I catch you playing with any more of them black specks of dirt, you'll be sorry. You understand?"

Johnny looked at his father, but didn't answer.

His father yelled. "*Do you understand?*"

Johnny seemed hesitant, but he finally spoke, his voice cracking. "I understand what you said, but I don't understand why I can't play ball with them."

"Because *I* said so, and because I won't have a weakling for a son."

"I'm not weak," Johnny said.

"I mean a weakling in the mind, boy. Somebody who doesn't have the guts to do what's best for society. For the good of others."

"But there's nothing wrong with Brandon. He's a nice guy; besides, he plays good ball."

"He's black, isn't he? That says it all."

"They got black people playing real baseball. So why can't I play ball with them?"

His father glared. He looked as if he would reach across the table and hit him, but he gritted his teeth and spoke slowly. "*Because. I. Said. So,*" he yelled. "That's reason enough. Do you understand that, or do I have to kick your ass?"

Johnny shook his head. "No, sir. I understand."

"Good, now finish your meal."

Michael finished his meal, had Johnny get him another beer, then said he was going out for a while.

"Drive safely," Sandy said as he left.

Michael laughed. "I know you wish I'd get killed, but don't worry, I won't."

Johnny helped his mother clean the table, and after his father left, he spoke quietly to his mother. "Why does Dad hate black people so much? And why does he curse so much and take God's name in vain? The nuns told us that's a mortal sin."

Sandy took the plates from Johnny and set them in the water to wash. As she scrubbed them clean, she sighed. "Who's to say, Johnny. Some people are just that way. They *shouldn't* be, but they are. And it's not just blacks. He hates Mexicans, Arabs, Chinese, gays . . . Hell, Johnny, he hates himself. I think that's the real problem."

"Why the heck did you marry him, Mom? You're not like that."

"No, and when I met your father, he wasn't either. At least, he didn't act like it. And he didn't curse like that either. I wouldn't have married him if he had."

"Is it because he drinks so much?"

Sandy sighed again. "It might be, Johnny. It just might be. I guess only your father and the Lord know why. I just wish someone would help him."

"Me too," Johnny said. "I'll say a prayer tonight. Maybe God will help."

Sandy wiped her soapy hands on the apron she wore, then rubbed Johnny's head. "That's a good idea, Johnny. God might just do that. Heaven knows, He's probably the only one who *can* help."

MORE TRAINING

2001, PARRIS ISLAND, SOUTH CAROLINA

Bentley looked Johnny in the eyes. He stared for a moment, and when he knew he had Johnny's full attention, he asked, "A family member taught you? As in an abusive or demanding father?"

Johnny almost fell off the stool. "What? No, my father—"

"Was probably a drunk," Bentley said. "Just like mine was."

When Bentley said that, Johnny felt more at ease. At that point, he decided it might be okay to open up a bit. It's not something he'd told many people; in fact, none, except the people who knew, like Uncle Dom and Aunt Clorinda.

"Want to grab a table?" Johnny asked Bentley.

Bentley picked up his beer and followed Johnny to a table near the corner, one that offered privacy.

"How'd you guess?" Johnny asked.

"Didn't take much," Bentley said. "I recognized all the signs. Not many kids learn to shoot like that unless they've been browbeaten or worse. I went through the same things for years. I don't have the physical scars to show for what my old man did, but I sure as hell have the mental ones."

Johnny nodded. "Same here. My Dad was a cop, and he knew exactly how, and where, to hit me so it didn't leave scars. No evidence."

"*Was* a cop?" Bentley asked.

Johnny didn't want to answer that question yet. It was too painful; instead, he just nodded. "Yeah, he was at the time."

"I got news for you, kid. There are a lot more people like you and me than you realize. And it's not a death sentence either. Fact is, if you learn to handle it right, it can be a blessing."

Johnny laughed. "I'd like to know how."

"The *how* is easy. Get your head out of your ass and stop feeling sorry for what happened, then recognize that whatever it was your old man or your uncle or your brother did to you was a gift."

"A gift?"

Bentley nodded. "That's right. Aren't many kids your age that can do what you can. Fact is, I'd bet good money there aren't any."

Johnny shrugged. "But what good is it?"

"It's a career, boy. Somebody who can shoot like you, can call your own shots. You can go to sniper school, get assigned damn near anywhere you want, do what you want. And when you're done—if you haven't fucked up—you can go to work anywhere you want in law enforcement: CIA, FBI, SWAT, anywhere."

Johnny perked up some. "You think so?"

"Shit, boy, I *know* so. I've been offered three jobs already. Damn good ones."

"So why haven't you taken them?"

Bentley took two sips of beer in succession and called for another. "Because I like what I do. I enjoy helping kids like you. I know what it feels like."

Johnny slugged his beer and ordered another as well. "All right, I'll give sniper school a shot and see if I like it."

Bentley smiled. "You will."

Bentley stayed for three more days, and he spent most of that time coaching Johnny. Not on mechanics. Johnny had that down pat, but he worked with him on mental conditioning and perseverance. Areas that required the wisdom of age, not the experience of repetitive practice.

He noticed great improvement in Johnny's confidence—even in three days—and he felt positive about his progress moving forward.

"You want to grab one beer before I head out?" Bentley asked.

"You're leaving tonight?"

Bentley nodded. "It's a long drive, and I prefer driving at night. A lot less traffic to contend with, and besides, it allows me to think about things. A lot of things."

"Sure. I'm up for a beer, but just one. Some ass has got me doing all kinds of shit to stay in shape."

Bentley laughed. "And you'll thank me for it if you ever have to sit still as a rock for days on end."

"I'll be ready," Johnny said. "I hope it doesn't happen, but I *will* be ready."

Johnny woke the next morning, charged up about his prospects. Bentley had laid out what was likely to happen—or at least be offered to him—and Johnny liked what he heard. The Marines were always looking for top shooters, and that was one area where Johnny excelled.

He completed the next week of training at the range, and they had moved the targets back to two hundred yards, which tested the skills much better. Many of the recruits who had done reasonably well at fifty, failed to even hit the target. This was especially true on windy days, despite the DI having warned them that wind greatly affects the accuracy of a shot.

Fortunately, Johnny had experience with not just shooting, but with adjusting his shot for velocity, windage, and knowing how to take the glare of the sun into account. At the end of the week, his targets couldn't be distinguished from the ones at fifty yards. He aced the shots.

Benz walked by just as Johnny finished up his shooting.

"Pretty good, McCoy, but don't get your head stuck up your ass just yet. You may be a good shot, but you haven't passed Basic, and I've seen a lot of good men pussy out in the second half."

Johnny snapped a salute. "Sergeant, yes Sergeant."

Benz knelt next to him and looked him in the eye. "Just keep your head straight, boy. You can handle the physical part. I see how big you are and how tough. But it's the mental things that get most people. When you think it couldn't get any worse, remember that thousands upon thousands upon thousands have done it before and made it. Hell, if they can do it, you can too."

"Sergeant, yes Sergeant. Thank you very much."

"You're welcome, McCoy. Now rest over the weekend and meditate or pray or do whatever the hell puts your mind at ease because you're going to need it to finish out the course."

"Sergeant, I enjoy facing obstacles like that as a challenge. It's sort of a test of will."

Benz stood and smiled. "I like hearing that. Keep that spirit, and this course won't be shit. You'll kick its ass."

"Thank you, Sergeant. I think so too."

"Don't get cocky, McCoy. After boot camp, you've got SOI, and its not for pussies either."

Johnny saluted. "Duly noted, Sergeant. I'll be ready."

Benz nodded and walked away. *I'll bet you will, boy.*

Johnny met a few of the guys at the pub that night, all of them sitting at a corner table. He ordered a beer and took the mug over to join them. "You look like a bunch of beat sons of bitches," he said. "Liven up. Let's play darts or pool or *something.*"

"We'd rather sit here and mope, McCoy. Not all of us are expert shots."

Johnny laughed as he pulled the chair across the wooden planks. "If you practiced, you could be. *And* if you listened to me."

"Screw you," Moj said. "I'll learn, but not by listening to you."

"You'll learn to miss," Danny said. "I'll take you up on that, McCoy. In fact, I already asked Benz, and he said if we got two or three people who were interested, he'd make time at the range for you to work with us."

"Be happy to," Johnny said. "Let me know when."

"I can't wait till Basic is over," Moj said. "Looking forward to getting a leave and seeing my folks."

"That leave will be short," Danny said. "Go home, kiss your mom, take a crap, then before you know it, you're on your way back."

Johnny laughed. "Short or not, I'll take it. But I don't have time to think about it. We've got a lot to go through before then."

"That ain't no shit," Moj said. "Some guys say it's the worst."

"I don't know if it'll be the worst, but you can bet it will be tough."

BASIC TRAINING IS OVER

The next week started out easy, but soon enough things changed. They did extensive field training, including three- and five-mile runs carrying full gear, scaling walls, climbing ropes, and more hiking than Johnny thought possible.

As they marched toward the barracks at the end of the day on Friday, Benz told them to rest up because the worst was yet to come. It wasn't what any of them wanted to hear, but it wasn't unexpected.

"Sounds like we're in deep shit," Moj said.

"Too deep for you, Moj," Danny said, and laughed.

During the next few weeks, they went through more than anyone had imagined. The worst of it, at least for Johnny, was the gas chamber. They put them in a closed room without masks and flooded it with tear gas.

They lined up outside the room, holding their gas masks, then DI Benz walked in front of them. "This drill is one of the more important ones. It may very well save your life one day, so pay attention and do it right."

"Sergeant, what is the exercise for?" Danny asked.

"Recruit, you should know better than to ask. You're lucky I'm in a good mood, or I'd make you go in there without a mask. Understand?"

"Sergeant, yes Sergeant."

"As I was saying, this is so you can experience what it's like to be under a gas attack, which you don't ever want to be. The gas we use has a name you morons couldn't pronounce, so I won't bother telling you what it is. Just know it won't kill you. It's the same gas the riot police use. What that means is it *will* make you tear up, it *will* make you sick to your stomach, it *will* make you cough like hell, and it *will* burn your skin." Benz laughed. "Other than that, it's a piece of cake."

Benz paced silently for a few seconds before speaking again. "This is gonna be the longest three to five minutes in your life. Before you come out of there, you'll wish you were dead. Actually, you'll wish you *had* died *before* going in there."

Benz slapped Moj playfully on the head. "Moj, you're gonna cry. I know it."

"No, Sergeant. I won't."

Benz laughed. "I'm betting you will, Moj. But don't worry, you won't be alone. You're going to learn what a mask is for, and you're going to learn how to get them out and put them on while under attack. *Is that clear?*" he yelled the last part.

"Yes, Sergeant," everyone shouted back.

Benz looked at his watch and grinned. "Good, then get ready. On the count of five, you go in."

The gas flooded the chamber, forcing the recruits to reach for the masks. Johnny fumbled with his, almost dropping it one time, but he eventually got it ready and put it on. It took him longer than he hoped, but he had survived. His skin burned, his throat burned, and he felt as if he'd been crying for days, but at least he could breathe. For a moment, it reminded him of when his father caught him smoking and put a paper bag over his head, then blew smoke through holes he'd made in the bag. He knew that wasn't as bad as this, but the memories he had told him differently.

When they finished, everybody rushed to get out of the chamber. It looked like people escaping a burning building. Once safely out, people bent over and rested their elbows on their thighs. Some men cried continually, but most just coughed and rubbed their skin where it burned.

"Oh, my God, that was nasty," Danny said. "I thought I was gonna die."

"I did die," Moj said. "I'm sure of it."

Between fits of coughing, Johnny managed to say, "Either way, we made it out, and despite what Moj might think, I believe we *are* alive."

Danny ran his hand up and down Johnny's face. "Yeah, I think you're right, Johnny."

Benz appeared out of nowhere, that shit-eating grin on his face. "You boys have fun? I told you it would be fun, didn't I?"

"Barrels of fun," Moj said.

"I'm glad," Benz said. "Now you're going to rest up for a few minutes before we go for a nice long walk to clear your lungs. Can't have you going to sleep with that nasty gas in there."

Johnny lifted his head and sighed. He waited until Benz was out of earshot, then whispered to Danny and Moj. "Anybody else want to throw that son of a bitch down a deep, deep hole right now?"

"Get me the shovel, and I'll start digging," Danny said.

Johnny and the rest of the unit stayed in the barracks that night, mostly telling tales of how bad things were in the chamber. "One thing's for sure," Danny said. "The worst has *got to* be over. I can't imagine a worse torture they could put us through than that."

A week later, Benz put Danny's theory to the test. They were led to the beach where the waves came in and told to lie on their backs. They were far enough in so when the water rolled in, it covered their heads, forcing them to hold their breath while the water continued in, then back out again, finally freeing them to breathe. It was a damn long time, and several of the men couldn't handle it. After being swamped by water a few times, they got up and walked out.

"Leave now and you may as well pack up to go home," Benz yelled.

Upon hearing that, a few of the men returned, but a few didn't. They became part of the ten or fifteen percent who don't make it through Basic. One thing Benz's threat did though, was inspire the rest of them to try harder. They held our breath a little longer each time, but it was getting tough to do so. Holding your breath for so long and so often was hard.

Johnny cursed at himself because he could have taken advantage of water activities when he lived with his aunt and uncle. He didn't though, because it reminded him of when his father used to hold his head under water in the tub until he couldn't breathe. It made him afraid of being under water. *Guess I'm paying the price now.*

It seemed as if the day would never end, but end it did, and Johnny was never so happy. On the way back to barracks, Benz moved alongside him.

"Looked like you were having trouble out there, McCoy."

Johnny nodded. "I was. I'm not used to being under water much. It was tough."

"Tough or not, you did good. I've seen the water break a lot of would-be Marines. Broke a few today. Some people swear the gas is worse, but it only lasts a few minutes. The bad part about this is how long it goes on. Be proud, boy. You did good."

"Thank you, Sergeant."

He returned to barracks and crashed on the mattress. Some of the guys were going to the pub, but he passed on that. "I'm too damn tired," he said. "I'm staying here."

A few of the other recruits stayed in barracks also, and most of them wrote letters to home or read letters from home. Johnny had a few to read, so he lay back, rested on a pillow, and opened them.

The first was from Aunt Clorinda. She asked the usual, the same every time. *'How are you, Johnny? Are you eating well? Are they being good to you?'*

Johnny laughed and put the letter back in the envelope, then he opened one from Tony. *'Hey, Johnny. When the hell are you coming home? I got nothing to do except kick Ronnie's ass. You need to come home so I can kick yours.'* Tony's letters weren't much different than Aunt Clorinda's. In content they were, but they were the same every time too.

The final letter was from Brandon. He hadn't expected one from him, but he was glad he'd written. *'Hey, white boy. How are you? I hope those Marines will finally be able to make a man out of you. God knows, I tried. But enough nonsense. The reason I'm writing is to see when you're coming home. My cousin Liz is staying with us for a few months and she's eager to meet you. I told her you were just an ordinary white boy, but she insists on seeing for herself. Anyway, give me a shout when you get back and we'll get together.'*

Johnny laughed to himself, then picked up a pen to respond. *'Don't try fooling me, black boy. Your cousin must be ugly if you want to fix her up with me, so I'm not falling for that shit. I will call when I get home, but don't count on me taking pity on your cousin Liz.'*

Johnny finished writing, stuffed the letter in an envelope and sealed it, then placed it in the to-be-mailed pile.

He was glad he'd stayed at the barracks. It felt good to hear from everyone.

FIRST LEAVE

Johnny and his fellow recruits had plenty more grueling exercises, a lot of them involving running with gear or swimming with gear, including an endurance training where they had to tread water while holding their rifles above their heads. There were also a few exercises geared toward escaping underwater scenarios, such as ships or planes that went down. It was easy to visualize the benefits to all of it, so it wasn't as tough to handle as some of the other exercises had been.

After a few more weeks of training, Benz announced everyone was eligible for ten days of leave. The news excited Johnny, and he made plans to head home to Cleveland. He could have waited and taken a bus, but he opted to spend a few of his hard-earned bucks and fly instead.

Once he landed, he called Brandon and asked if he could pick him up. An hour later, Brandon arrived, and he had someone with him. Johnny got in, tossing his bag in the back seat and sitting with it. A beautiful young woman sat in the passenger seat, and when

Johnny got in, she turned and smiled, extending her hand as she did.

"My name is Liz," she said. "You must be the white boy."

Johnny laughed when she said that. "So I see you really *are* Brandon's cousin. And I thought he was lying."

"He lied about one thing," Liz said.

"What's that?" Johnny asked.

"He said you were good-looking. I think he exaggerated."

Johnny laughed. "Really? Maybe we should talk more about this at the movies, or over dinner at Jasper's."

"Well, well," Liz said. "Jasper's it is. But you better bring a silver tongue. I'm hard to convince."

"No problem," Johnny said. "The lighting is good at Jasper's, so you'll be able to see for yourself."

Liz smiled at Johnny. "When do you want to go?"

"How about tomorrow night? Seven o'clock."

"I'll be ready," Liz said.

"Brandon's house?"

"That's where I'm staying."

"I *am* in the car, you know," Brandon said. "We're halfway home and no one has said a word to me yet."

"Hi, Brandon," Johnny said.

"Fuck you, asshole. But hey, you want to try to get up a game tomorrow?"

"A baseball game?" Johnny asked.

"I don't care. Baseball or basketball. One or the other."

"I doubt we'll find enough people for two full teams, but we might for a game of hoops."

"All right," Brandon said. "I'll make the calls when I get home. Plan on it by ten, maybe earlier."

"St. Edmonds?" Johnny asked.

"You got it," Brandon said. "Losers buy lunch."

"Hope you got enough money," Johnny said. "I don't intend to lose."

"And the road to hell is paved with good intentions," Brandon said. "Just bring your money because you'll need it."

Brandon's team won the game sixty-eight to sixty-one, and Johnny and his boys had to fork over the dough for lunch. After eating, Brandon gave Johnny a ride home, and they chatted. "Johnny, one thing about Liz . . ."

"Don't worry, Brandon. I'll be a gentleman."

"No, not that. I doubt if you've heard, but since you've been away, there's been some lunatic in the city who's killing young black girls. I wanted to warn you."

"What? I hadn't heard. How long has this been going on?"

"Just started a couple of months ago, but the guy's already killed two people. Both black and both around twenty years old. He's also sent a note to the paper saying there will be more to come."

"They've got no leads?" Johnny asked. "No suspects?"

Brandon shook his head. "They say they don't, but who knows? I doubt if they're looking hard. It's only black girls being killed."

Johnny looked over at Brandon. He wanted to tell him there's no way the cops would be like that. He *wanted* to, but he couldn't. He knew damn right well that may be *exactly* what was happening. After all, his father had been a cop, and he hated black people more than anything. *If there's one rotten apple, there could easily be more.*

BACK TO JOHNNY'S YOUTH

1995—CLEVELAND, OHIO

Johnny ate breakfast and left the house early. He hoped to get away clean, but he was pretty sure his father would follow him. He got about four blocks away and cut through a neighbor's yard to the street behind them. When he hopped over the fence, he looked both ways and thought for sure he saw his father's car. *Just like I thought.*

Instead of heading to St. Edmonds for a pickup game, he detoured to the arcade to play a few of the new video games and some older pinball machines. His cousin Ronnie was playing Space Invaders when he showed up. Johnny tapped him on the shoulder. "Ronnie, do me a solid. Check out front and see if you spot my father. I'll play the game for you."

"Shit, Johnny, I got a good game going," Ronnie said.

"Don't worry about it. You know you're not as good as me. Now get out there and check for me. And don't get seen."

Ronnie returned in a few minutes. "He was there all right, but he left a minute ago."

"You're sure he's gone?" I asked.

"I saw him leave, for Christ's sake. He's gone. Now step aside and give me my game."

"You mean *games* as in plural. I already won you a free one, so eat shit."

Ronnie laughed. "Thanks, Johnny. See ya' later."

Johnny left the arcade and headed to St. Edmonds, where he joined an ongoing basketball game. He joined Brandon's team, and they won handily, putting a smile on Brandon's face.

"Damn, I didn't know white boys could play so good. You're not bad, Johnny. Not good, but not bad."

"Shit. A couple of one-on-ones will show you who's not good," Johnny said.

"You're right about that," Brandon said. "But I don't want to embarrass you. And by the way, how did you get out without your psycho father tracking you down?"

Johnny laughed. "It was tough, but I managed. My cousin, Ronnie, helped me."

"Your father is one scary dude," Brandon said. "Even more scary when you know he's a cop. And you wonder why us black people are afraid of cops? It's because they'll kill you, that's why."

Johnny played ball for several more hours, and then he stopped at the arcade and hung out for a while. At the end of day, Johnny went home and walked in the door wearing a smile.

His father stood in the hallway, hands on hips and glaring. "Where the hell have you been, boy?"

"At the arcade," Johnny said.

"Bullshit, I saw you playing ball with that nigger."

"You're dreaming," Johnny said. "I was at the arcade. Ask Ronnie. Go ahead and call him. We played Space Invaders and Asteroids all day."

"Maybe I will," his father said, in an obvious attempt to bluff. He picked up the phone and dialed, but before anyone picked up, he hung up the receiver. "Okay, boy. I'm gonna believe you this time, but *only* this time. If I find out you lied, your ass is mine. You hear?"

"I *hear*, but I didn't lie. I was at the arcade. Where were you? At the bar?"

Michael reached over and smacked Johnny with the back of his hand, knocking him off the chair onto the floor.

"Michael!" Johnny's mother yelled, then Michael smacked her too. Johnny charged him and head butted his gut, taking his breath away, but not for long. He reached down and grabbed the back of Johnny's shirt, picked him up, and threw him across the floor. "Do that again, boy, and I might have to kill you."

"Michael!" Sandy said. "May God strike you dead if you say anything like that again. He's your son."

"Woman, God isn't striking anyone dead, and He isn't doing anything else either. God quit intervening in shit a thousand years ago—*if* He did it then."

Johnny helped his mother with the dishes, then he went to his room to read. There was no sense staying downstairs with them.

About an hour later, his door cracked open, and his father walked in. It was obvious he'd been drinking heavily from the way he walked and the smell of liquor.

"You awake, boy?"

69

"I'm reading," Johnny said.

Michael sat on the edge of the bed, grabbed the book from Johnny's hands, and tossed it across the room. "Your mother saved your ass tonight, but she won't always be there. The next time you disrespect me, you'll pay a price. A damn big price. You understand?"

Johnny looked up and nodded. He wanted to tell him 'go to hell' or 'I don't care what price I pay,' but the truth was, Johnny did care. For better or worse—and it was usually worse—he *was* his father. And Johnny had to live with that. "Yes, sir," he said.

Michael smiled and tousled Johnny's hair. "Okay, good. Now go to sleep."

AN UNNECESSARY KILLING

Michael always used targets of black people at the shooting range. Sometimes, when he had to stop at his friend's house to pick up some extra loads, he'd come out with a handful of new targets as well. The pictures might be different, but they were always of black people and they always showed the heart as the target.

One time, Johnny asked him why he bothered. "Why do you pay for those targets? They give you free targets at the range."

"They don't have the targets I want," Michael said.

"Isn't a plain old target just as good, Dad?" Johnny asked.

"Depends on what you're aiming for, boy. If you're aiming for the heart, ain't nothing like a target that shows that. And these targets all show the heart."

"But why are you always aiming at black people, Dad?"

His father turned to him and scowled. "Because they're the scum of the earth, boy. They're lower than whale shit. You need to learn that, and you need to learn it now. Hear me?"

"Yes, sir," Johnny said. "One more question, Dad. If it's okay."

"Of course, it's okay. What do you need?"

"Why do you buy shells from that man we just visited? Why not use the ones at the range?"

"The ones at the range will do, but they're not as good as PJ's loads. Nobody can load a shell like PJ," he said, and laughed.

Johnny shot well at the range that day, and they ended up staying longer than usual. To his surprise, there was no yelling and no smacking. It turned out to be a pleasant day.

Johnny did his chores when he got home, then he ate dinner and went upstairs to read. In the morning, he once again sneaked out to the arcade, then on to St. Edmonds to play ball. He loved playing ball, whether it was basketball or baseball.

All week long, Johnny used the same scheme to get away from his father's watchful eyes. He'd go to the arcade, where Ronnie or Tony or someone else he trusted were almost always playing games, then he'd get them to watch for his father until he was gone. He'd wait a few minutes, then hustle to St. Edmonds and join Brandon for a game of hoops or baseball, depending on how many people they had.

On Saturday, his father was off work and had time to kill. He followed Johnny to the arcade and went through the normal routine of checking out he was there. But this time, when he drove away, he circled the block and waited a few minutes. Then he saw Johnny leave the arcade and head to St. Edmonds.

Michael kept his distance and followed Johnny until he saw him playing basketball with a bunch of jungle bunnies. *Son of a bitch. That son of a bitch. After all I told him, and he goes and does this. He'll pay. He'll goddamn pay, all right.*

It was almost dinner time when Johnny opened the front door and announced he was home. "What's for dinner, Mom? I'm starved," he said as he entered the kitchen.

"You should be as hard as you played all day," his father said.

Johnny looked at his father with skepticism. "What do you mean?"

"I mean, it's tiring playing basketball all day. All that running and jumping and all."

"I was at the arcade," Johnny said.

Michael grabbed a handful of Johnny's hair and pulled him over. "Arcade, huh? You lying son of a bitch. I *saw* you at St. Edmonds, and you were playing basketball with a bunch of damn jungle bunnies. In fact, I'm surprised some of it didn't rub off on you. Filthy bastards that they are."

Johnny's head hurt, but he couldn't pull away. "Dad, you're hurting me."

"Good. Maybe now you'll listen to me when I tell you I don't want you hanging around with them scum."

"Michael!" Sandy yelled. "Let the boy go. You're hurting him."

"That's my job, woman. So shut the hell up."

Sandy grabbed a frying pan from the counter and stormed across the kitchen floor. She lifted it as if she would strike him. "Let him go, or I swear I'll hit you."

Michael laughed. "You'll do no such thing. Now put the pan down and shut up."

Sandy turned as if she were going back to cook, then she spun quickly and hit him, but he must have seen it coming because he raised his arm to block it. The only good thing is when he raised his arm, he let go of Johnny, and Johnny ran.

"Goddamn!" Michael yelled when the pan hit the back of his forearm. "You son of a bitch. That hurt."

"It was supposed to," Sandy said. "Now you know some of what Johnny feels."

Michael stood quickly and reached for Sandy. "And now *you're* gonna know," he said.

Sandy moved back and swung the pan again, but he swatted it away and knocked it from her hand.

She ran, but he grabbed the back of her dress and yanked her back. Sandy panicked. She knew he'd hurt her now. She looked around for something to hit him with and saw a knife on the countertop. She grabbed the handle, turned, and stabbed him in the side, just above the waist.

"Son of a bitch!" Michael yelled. "Son of a goddamn bitch! You're gonna pay for this now, woman. I'm gonna kill you."

Sandy still gripped the knife, and she crouched and held it in a threatening position. "You come any closer, and I'll put this in your heart."

Michael stopped moving toward her, then he stood straight and pulled out a gun. "That knife ain't shit now, woman."

"Dad, no!" Johnny screamed from the other room and ran into the kitchen, ramming into his father's back.

Michael reached behind him with his left hand and tossed Johnny to the side with no more than a glance. It was almost as if he were swatting a fly. He then raised the gun and pointed it at Sandy "Put that knife down and do it now."

Sandy made no move to put it down; instead, she gritted her teeth and said, "Get out of my house and don't ever come back. I should have thrown you out long ago, but I'm doing it now."

"The hell you are," Michael said.

"The hell I am is right," Sandy said. "Now get out."

Michael didn't move, so Sandy reached for him with the knife. When she did, Michael fired the weapon, hitting her in the chest, close to the heart. Sandy gasped, dropped the knife, and grabbed her chest as she fell.

"Mom! Mom, no!" Johnny yelled and ran toward her, tears already flowing. He knelt next to his mother, who had blood pouring from her wound, and tried hugging her. He cried uncontrollably. "Mom. Mom."

She attempted to speak, but then her head fell to the side and hit the floor.

"Oh, my God," Johnny yelled. "My God. She's dead. You killed Mom." He jumped up, grabbed the knife, and ran for his father, who just stood there staring. Before Johnny reached him, he lifted the gun, placed it under his chin, and pulled the trigger.

The shot startled and scared Johnny. At first, he thought his father had shot at him. Then his father fell, and Johnny saw the blood. So much blood. He screamed again and ran. He ran out the front door and kept running.

Two houses down the street, Mrs. Banning grabbed hold of him. "Johnny, is everything all right? I heard gunshots."

"He killed her," Johnny said through heavy sobbing. "He killed my mom."

Mrs. Banning stood and gasped. "Your mother is dead? Oh, my God! Who killed her?"

"My father," Johnny said. "He shot her." He then wrapped his arms around Mrs. Banning and squeezed. "What am I gonna do? Mom's dead."

Mrs. Banning led him into her house. "Don't worry about that now, Johnny. We'll call the ambulance."

She led Johnny to a chair, got him some water to drink, then called the police. She whispered when she spoke. "Tell them to send an ambulance too. The boy said she's dead, but I don't know."

WORST DAY EVER

Johnny sat with Mrs. Banning for at least an hour. He saw the police car arrive, followed by an ambulance. Then two more police cars pulled up. Soon, an officer knocked on her door, and she showed them inside.

The officer introduced himself as Lenny DiMarco, then knelt in front of Johnny and spoke softly. "Johnny, isn't it?"

Johnny nodded. He had stopped crying a while ago, but he still found it hard to talk. "I'm sure you don't remember, but I met you about a year ago at your Uncle Dom's house. You were playing with his kids in the backyard and my son joined you. His name was Lou. Lou DiMarco."

Johnny nodded again, but said nothing.

"Johnny, I'm so sorry about what happened. Did you see it? Can you tell me what happened?"

"My dad shot Mom. He killed her, then shot himself."

"He shot your mom? Do you know why?"

"Because he was hurting me, so Mom yelled at him and told him to quit. When he wouldn't, she swung a pan at him."

"And that's when he shot her?"

Johnny shook his head. "He went after her and was hurting her, so she grabbed a knife and stabbed him. That's when he shot her."

Officer DiMarco nodded. "Then what?"

"Then I charged him, but he put the gun under his chin and killed himself. I'm glad he did."

"I'm sure you don't mean that, Johnny. No one wants to see—"

"I mean it, all right. He was mean to me and Mom. He was always hitting us and yelling at us. All he did was drink."

DiMarco looked up and saw Mrs. Banning standing behind Johnny and nodding.

"Okay, Johnny. I'm so sorry, but how about I call your Uncle Dom and have him come get you?"

Johnny nodded again. "Yeah. Do that. I like Uncle Dom."

The officer walked into the kitchen and moved close to Mrs. Banning. "May I use the phone, ma'am?"

"Of course, officer. And for what it's worth, what the boy told you is true. His father was a monster. Always drinking and yelling. You could hear him all the way down the block. And he hit the boy all the time."

"Why didn't someone report it?"

"Are you kidding me? Several of us reported it a number of times, but no one did anything. Sometimes they'd send a patrol car out to investigate, but as soon as they found out he was a cop, they let it slide. Gave him a verbal warning is all they did."

"You saw this?"

"Not only saw it and heard it, but Sandy, the boy's mother, told me about it too. He'd swear he just had a few too many, and that he wouldn't do it again, and they'd let him go. Next week, he'd be right back at it."

"All right, thanks, ma'am. Can he stay with you until his uncle arrives? He seems comfortable here."

"No problem for me. I'm happy to look out for the boy. And I know Dom, so just tell him Johnny's at Mrs. Banning's house. He knows where I live."

"Yes, ma'am," DiMarco said, then tipped his hat and walked outside.

Ten minutes later, Dominic Camino pulled up, his wife, Clorinda, in the car with him. He jumped out and ran for the house. Lenny DiMarco stood on the sidewalk close to the street.

"Dom, Johnny's inside. He's pretty shaken up obviously. Saw the whole thing go down."

"I knew that no-good son of a bitch would do something like this. I *knew* it. I told her to leave him a dozen times, but she wouldn't do it because of the church."

"I'm sorry, Dom. I know what it's like to lose a little sister."

Clorinda held onto Dom and patted his back. "Come on, dear. Let's get in there with Johnny."

Dom and Clorinda opened the door and walked in slowly. Clorinda ran to Johnny when she saw him. Johnny got up and hugged her. When he did, he began crying again, and he cried hard, so hard he couldn't stop.

Dom walked up behind them and placed his hand on Johnny's back. He looked as if he didn't know what to do. "It's okay, buddy. It's okay. Aunt Clorinda and I will take you home with us."

"Where will I sleep?" Johnny asked.

Dom almost laughed. "Don't worry about sleep, buddy. We'll figure that out. If you have to, you can sleep in Tony and Ronnie's room until we get something else. That okay?"

Johnny nodded, but he didn't let go of Aunt Clorinda; in fact, he squeezed harder.

After a few minutes, Dom tapped Clorinda on the back of the head and gestured for her to take Johnny outside. Once she did, he called his house and told the boys what happened and said Johnny would be coming home to stay for a while. Maybe a long while.

He hung up the phone, thanked Mrs. Banning, then went outside where Clorinda and Johnny were sitting in the car. Dom got in the front seat. "All right," he said. "Let's get this show on the road."

"Dom!" Clorinda said.

Dom nodded. "Sorry, I didn't mean to be disrespectful." He turned toward the back seat where Johnny sat before pulling away from the curb. "I called Tony and Ronnie before leaving. They're getting hot dogs out so we can grill some. That okay?"

Johnny nodded, still sobbing. "Fine."

As Dom pulled into the street, Clorinda reached over and squeezed his hand. When he looked at her, she mouthed. "I'm so sorry, honey."

He nodded and squeezed her hand back.

On the ride to home to see Ronnie and Tony, Johnny thought about how his life had changed. It was the worst day of his life, and he couldn't imagine living without his mom. But he was glad his dad wouldn't be around. He knew it wasn't nice to think such things, but it was true. His dad had been an evil man. His mother had said it was the drinking, but Johnny didn't know. *I don't think drinking can make you that bad. He must have been bad to begin with.*

BACK TO THE GRIND

SUMMER, 2001. CAMP LEJEUNE, NORTH CAROLINA

Michael took a bus back to base. He wasn't as eager to return as he was to get away; besides, money was a factor. He'd unexpectedly spent a lot going out with Liz. She offered to pay each time, but Johnny wouldn't hear of it. His wad of bills shrank each time they went someplace, but what the heck, that's what money was for.

He smiled as he remembered the nights on the town. They went to the movies, to a play, to a local carnival, and to dinner a *lot*. Too many times. The tickets for the play were pricey because Johnny insisted on good seats, but it was the dinners that ate up most of his cash. *I'll just have to get lucky playing cards with the guys.*

He had plenty to think about on his ride, but mostly he thought about how different it would be at Camp Lejeune, in North Carolina. It seemed as if every waking moment was spent on speculation of how things would change.

But if every *waking* moment was spent on Camp Lejeune, then every dreaming moment was spent thinking of Liz. He hadn't been gone six hours, and he already dreamed of spending time with her again. He knew he liked Liz, and not just because he dreamed about her, but because the dreams made him feel good.

The grinding sound of brakes—metal-on-metal—caused Johnny to wake. He looked out the windows and could tell by the terrain that they had left Ohio and were likely getting close to their destination. His mood changed from anxiousness to anticipation as he thought of seeing some of his new friends, especially Danny and Moj.

Some of the guys worried this part of training would be as bad as boot camp, but Johnny knew it wouldn't. That's not saying it would be a piece of cake. He knew there would be plenty of brutal exercises and drills, and there would be even more underwater drills (and torture), but there would also be a lot of range shooting. And *that* he looked forward to.

Sometime around six that night, the bus pulled into Camp Lejeune. The doors opened and a couple handfuls of Marines got off, most toting at least a small pack of clothes and toiletries.

As he stepped off the bus, he heard a familiar sound. "Fall in!"

Johnny almost laughed. All drill sergeants sounded the same, and this one was no different.

"My name is Sergeant Blackwood. I'm going to be your mother, your father, and your worst nightmare for the foreseeable future. Is that understood?"

"Yes, Sergeant," everyone answered.

"Have you all lost your voices? I can't hear you," Blackwood said.

"Sergeant, yes Sergeant." This time, everyone shouted.

"One thing to know before you go to barracks. You are no longer little pussies in boot camp. You are now *big* pussies, and you belong to me. You will do what I say, when I say it, and there will be no hesitation. Is *that* understood?"

"Sergeant, yes Sergeant," echoed through the camp.

The first week was a piece of cake when compared to Basic, though Johnny figured as much before he got to camp. But the next two weeks picked up the pace with both physical and mental tests. During one extended hike with full gear, Danny ran up alongside Johnny. He looked behind him, then spoke in a lowered voice.

"You see that big fucking Alabama hick back there? The one with muscles growing on muscles?"

"You mean Alabama *tick,* don't you?" Moj asked. "His fuckin' head is no bigger than a pin compared to his body."

"Either way, he's a big motherfucker," Danny said. "And a pain in the ass, to boot. He's always giving everybody a lot of shit."

"If he gives Johnny any shit, he'll just shoot his ass," Moj said.

"Yeah, and from the other side of the camp," Danny said. "The tick won't know what hit him."

"Just tell Blackwood," Johnny said. "He'll take him down like a piñada."

"Sure, McCoy. We rat out a fellow Marine, and we'll be toast. The fuckin' roaches will get more respect."

"I gave you an option," Johnny said. "Take it or deal with the consequences."

A week later, Blackwood called for the first underwater escape exercise. It was a simulated helicopter crash where the unit was quickly sinking. Teams of four Marines had to unbuckle and get out of the copter and away from the crash site, and they had to do it all without breathing apparatus. A successful mission required a person to hold their breath for a long time—upwards of two minutes.

During the escape, the Tick grabbed Danny's ankle as he swam to the surface, holding him under. Danny struggled for twenty or thirty seconds until Cal finally let him go. He broke the surface, opened his mouth, and breathed deeply.

After swimming to the shore, Danny grabbed his gear and sat facing the water while holding his firearm. Cal surfaced a few seconds later and found himself looking down the barrel of a pistol.

"You're a dead motherfucker," Danny said.

"Whoa! Ease up, Marine. I was just messing with you."

"That's fine, Cal. But I'm not messing with you."

"Come on, Danny. Put the gun down. it was just a joke."

Danny's hands shook, but he held the gun firmly.

Johnny surfaced a short way down, swam to shore, then headed up the beach. He slowed when he saw Danny holding a gun on Cal. "Danny, take it easy, bud. Put the gun down and relax."

"I'll put it down after I use it," Danny said. "I'm putting that motherfucker in the ground."

Johnny approached slowly, his hands in the air. "Danny, remember all the shit we went through in Basic? Don't make all that for nothing. Don't throw it away over an asshole like this."

Danny raised the gun a bit and held it tightly.

"Don't do it, Danny," Johnny said. "It's not worth it. I promise you, it's not."

Danny lowered and raised the gun several times. It was apparent he was torn about what to do. Johnny got within a few feet of him and held out his hand, palm up. "Come on, Danny. Hand it over. And do it before Blackwood shows up. Nobody wants that shit storm."

Cal stood still as a rock until Danny finally lowered the gun. "You're one lucky son of a bitch, Cal. If not for Johnny, I'd have put a bullet in your fucking brain—if you have one."

Cal waited for Johnny to take the gun, then he sneered. "You don't have the balls to do anything, Danny boy. Next time, I'll hold you under till you drown."

Danny started to get up, but Johnny held him down. "Forget about it, Dan. He's not worth it; besides, here comes Blackwood."

Blackwood walked up and got in Danny's face. "Did I see you holding a firearm on another Marine?"

Danny didn't say anything, so I spoke up. "No, Sergeant. It was a joke. And the gun wasn't loaded."

"So if I pluck his firearm from his side and inspect it, I'll find it empty?"

"Sergeant, yes will. You can pull it out and fire it at me. It's empty."

Blackwood looked from Danny to Johnny to Cal, then he nodded. "I'll buy that line today, gentlemen, but don't push it. Next time, I may take you up on your dare."

Johnny saluted. "Sergeant, yes Sergeant."

"Now get your asses back to barracks. We have a busy day tomorrow."

LETTERS FROM HOME

Johnny walked out of the shower and was busy drying off when mail-call was announced. He finished up quickly and got in line just in time to receive his letters from home—and he had a few. One from Aunt Clorinda, one from Ronnie and Tony, and one from Liz. He opened the one from Liz first.

Dear Johnny:

It's been way too long. I miss you and want you home. I wanted to go to the theater the other night, but realized I had no one to go with. And I haven't enjoyed a meal since you returned. You've got to come back or I'll wither away to nothing, and I know you don't want that. You said you didn't like girls who were extra skinny.

Anyway, know that I'm sitting in my room feeling lonely every night and waiting for you to come home. In the meantime, I've sent you a picture of me to keep your mind off other women. And no, it's not that kind of picture.

Johnny stared at her picture and smiled. She stood in front of a big oak tree near the park, one they enjoyed sitting under on the park bench. She had the prettiest dark brown eyes, and her hair sparkled.

He put her picture in his wallet, making sure to tuck it in so it didn't crease or wrinkle.

Johnny pulled a pen and paper from his bedside stand and began to write a response.

As he started, Cal walked up behind him and peered over his shoulder. "Writing to someone, Johnny?"

"Just answering letters," he said.

"Who you writing to? A girlfriend?"

Johnny nodded without looking up. "Yeah, my girlfriend."

"Tough to keep a girlfriend when you're in service," Cal said.

"Ain't that the truth," Johnny said.

"She a looker?" Cal asked.

"I think so, yeah."

"You got a picture?"

Johnny looked up and saw Cal looked serious. "Sure," he said, and pulled Liz's photo out of his wallet.

Cal looked at the picture and laughed. "A spook? You're going out with a goddamn spook?" He held up the picture and turned to the rest of the barracks. "Hey, guys. Look at this. Old Johnny boy is dating a spook."

There were two black guys in the barracks, but neither one of them said anything. Johnny stood up and reached to grab the picture from Cal, but he yanked it away.

"Oh, no. You're not getting it back yet. I may want a piece of this black ass when I go on leave next time. *If* she can handle what I got," Cal said, and reached down and squeezed his genitals.

Johnny's blood boiled. He balled his fist, then swung and hit Cal square in the jaw. Next, he hit him with two kidney jabs, dropping him to the ground. Cal lay on the floor gasping for air, but Johnny wasn't done with him. Not yet. He got on top of Cal and pummeled his face, one punch after another, until blood poured from his mouth and nose.

A moment later, the DI burst through the door. "What the hell is going on?"

"Ten-Hut," a recruit yelled, and everyone snapped to attention.

"Get the hell up," the DI said, addressing Johnny and Cal.

"One of you better have a damn good explanation for what I witnessed."

"Sergeant, yes Sergeant," Johnny said. "My fault, Sergeant. I threw the first punch."

"And why did you do it?" Blackwood asked.

"Sergeant, I'd rather not say."

"I don't give three fucks if you'd rather not, you'll tell me or you'll wish you'd died."

"I was making fun of his girl," Cal said. "It wasn't his fault. I'd have done the same thing he did."

Blackwood grabbed hold of Cal's face and turned it from side to side. "Looks like you put a beating on Cal, Johnny. He must have said something bad about your girl."

Blackwood stepped over in front of Johnny and got within inches of his face. "But I don't care what he said about her. You don't strike a fellow Marine. Got that?"

"Sergeant, yes Sergeant."

"Good, now report to the shrink first thing. His name is Rutger —*Captain* Rutger. He may laugh it off, or he may kick you out. His choice."

"Sergeant, yes Sergeant."

As Blackwood turned to leave, everyone saluted again.

When Johnny woke, he had his coffee, then breakfast, then went to visit the shrink, Dr. Rutger.

After a brief introduction, Rutger pestered him about the beating. "That was pretty severe for something as simple as making a comment about your girl," Rutger said.

"Sir, what he said was uncalled for."

"What did he say?"

Johnny hesitated before realizing he had to answer. "Made fun of her ancestry, Captain." Johnny said.

"I think you're going to have to be more specific," Dr. Rutger said.

"He called her a spook, sir."

"So she's black?"

"Sir, yes sir."

"He could have said worse, you know."

"If he did, the beating would have been worse, sir."

Rutger looked as if he would laugh. "Why did it bother you so much, Johnny?" He shuffled a few papers on his desk. "Is it because of how your father was? Did he not like black people?"

Johnny thought back to those days so long ago, so very long. And he thought back to the day his father killed his mom. He'd never forget that day, and he'd never forget what he thought about his father. His mother had said the drinking made his father do bad things. Johnny remembered *exactly* what he thought about that.

I don't think drinking can make you that bad. He must have been bad to begin with.

Now he worried he may have inherited some of that meanness. Most of all, he didn't want the shrink to think he was crazy. If the shrink thought that, he might discharge him, and Johnny couldn't have that. Not that.

A NEW LIFE

SIX YEARS AGO (1995)—CLEVELAND, OHIO

Aunt Clorinda turned toward Johnny, who was lying on the back seat of the car. "Johnny, I know things seem horrible right now, but they'll get better with time. And now you'll be staying at our house, so at least you'll be with people you know."

"And you'll have Ronnie and Tony to hang with too," Uncle Dom said. "Don't forget that. I know you guys get along, right?"

Johnny nodded, but barely. All he could do was think of life with no mom. *What am I going to do?*

"You know, Johnny, I think Aunt Clorinda was right earlier. I think you should stay with Ronnie and Tony in their room for a while. You guys will have a good time." Dom wagged a finger at Johnny. "But no damn sneakin' down and watching TV after bedtime. Got that?"

Johnny tried not to, but he grinned. Uncle Dom had caught them several times doing just that when Johnny spent the night a few times. "We won't, Uncle Dom. I promise."

Dom pulled up to the house a few minutes later, and Aunt Clorinda helped Johnny out of the car and walked him inside. I know you don't have anything with you, but Uncle Dom will go over later and get your clothes and toothbrush and such. Right now, there are a lot of people there.

Johnny nodded. "No problem. I don't need anything."

Aunt Clorinda gave a brief chuckle. "Everyone needs something, Johnny, but I know what you mean. We'll make do until we get your stuff."

Tony and Ronnie ran out the front door to greet Johnny, and both of them told him how sorry they were.

"It was terrible," Johnny said. "The worst thing I ever saw."

Ronnie held his hands over his ears and walked away. "Don't tell me about it," he said. "I don't want to hear."

"You mean your dad killed your mom?" Tony asked.

Johnny nodded. "Right in the kitchen," he said, and began crying again.

"Darn," Tony said. "He must have been crazy."

Despite what his father had done, Johnny's reaction was to come to his father's defense. Then he thought about it and realized Tony was right—his father *was* crazy.

The next few months went by slowly, slower than any time in Johnny's life. Every day, he missed his mom. He even missed his dad, and he hated himself for doing so. Why should he miss a sick man like that? The man who had killed his mother.

The only sign of hope is that Aunt Clorinda seemed to have been right about time. The more time that passed, the better Johnny felt. He didn't actually feel better about what happened, and he still missed his mom every day, but he thought about it less. And when he wasn't thinking about it, he could have fun. Real fun, like playing ball with Ronnie and Tony or going down to meet Brandon for a pickup game of hoops at St. Edmonds.

Sometimes, mostly at nights, those thoughts made him feel guilty. Like he was forgetting his mom. He even talked to Aunt Clorinda about it one morning when he got up early, before Tony or Ronnie.

She patted the top of his head, then kissed his forehead. "That's nothing to worry about, Johnny. It's God's way of letting people heal. A person can't live with so much grief, so God let's them have time to grieve, then he slowly makes them forget. It happens to everybody."

Johnny looked up at Aunt Clorinda with hope showing in his eyes. "Really?" he asked. "For real, Aunt Clorinda?"

She hugged Johnny again and whispered to him. "For real, Johnny. You know I'd never lie to you."

Johnny cried softly. "I love you, Aunt Clorinda. Uncle Dom too."

She squeezed him tighter. "We love you too, Johnny, and we always will."

1997

For the next few years, things did get better, just like Aunt Clorinda said they would. Johnny slowly forgot the horrible thing his father did, yet he held onto the loving memories he had of his mother. He grew to be close friends with his cousins, but also with

97

Brandon, whom he had grown to like a lot. Brandon had a good sense of humor, not to mention he was a good ballplayer.

On his thirteenth birthday, Uncle Dom surprised Johnny by taking off work and going to the park with all of them to play ball. Dom didn't play, but he did act as a ref. Afterward, they went home to shower and change clothes, then Uncle Dom took them to the early movie showing.

There was another surprise waiting when Johnny got home. Uncle Dom and Aunt Clorinda had invited a bunch of people over for a party, including his father's brother Bob and his wife, Trudy, as well as his brother Harry and his wife, Sarah. It was good to see everyone.

After a couple hours of partying, Johnny went upstairs with Ronnie and Tony, while the rest of them gathered in the backyard and talked. The bedroom window was open though, and Johnny heard everything they said.

"The boy's getting big," Bob said. "I can't believe he's so tall."

"He's got his father's genes, I'll say that," Trudy said.

"Let's hope he didn't get them all," Harry said. "Mike was bat-shit crazy, but I guess everyone knows that now."

"I think most people knew it before then," Sarah said. "I told you and Bob that the first time I met him, and that was early on."

"Don't act like you knew something we didn't," Bob said. "Hell, I was the one who called it in anonymously to the department years ago, but they didn't do shit about it."

Harry shook his head. "I hate to say it, but I'm glad he's gone. Just a damn shame that Sandy had to go with him."

Johnny reached over and quietly closed the window. He didn't need to hear any more about his father; he already *knew* his father was crazy. *He was a crazy, racist, lunatic, son of a bitch—that's what he was.*

CAMP LEGEUNE

Everybody talks about a Marine's Basic Training and how difficult it is, but no one talks much about the continuation of training, and that is almost as difficult. Not so much physically draining because if a person makes it through boot camp, their body has been somewhat conditioned. There are still physical challenges, to be sure, but the mental preparedness is worse. It's tough to explain how difficult it can be. The physical challenges are ever present though such as taking twenty kilometer hikes with full gear (98 pounds). And one of Johnny's already mentioned nightmares—underwater escape scenarios—of which there were many.

Johnny sweated out all week, waiting for Rutger to come down on him for the incident with Cal. On Friday, Sergeant Blackwood informed Johnny that Dr. Rutger wanted to see him at end of day.

Johnny snapped a salute. "Sergeant, did Dr. Rutger specify a time?"

"End of day," Sergeant Blackwood said.

When his unit was dismissed for the day, Johnny ran all the way to see Rutger. He opened the door, saluted, and announced himself.

"Sir, Private McCoy, as requested, sir." Then he stood at attention and waited to be acknowledged.

Captain Rutger finished what he was writing, placed the papers on his desk to the side, then looked up at Johnny. "At ease, Private. I called you here to discuss what happened between you and your fellow Marine."

"Sir, yes sir."

"I'm not in favor of violence as a means of solving disputes; in fact, I abhor violence of all types. You might think that odd coming from a Marine, but it's true."

"Yes, sir."

"Now that I've said all that, I must say that I'm not in favor of racist comments either. Your fellow Marine was definitely in the wrong, and he needed discipline. However, it was not your place to administer that discipline. Is that understood, Private?"

"Sir, yes sir."

"If you think you can continue without exhibiting any more violent behavior, I think we can forget this happened."

Johnny's smile stretched so wide it hurt. "Sir, yes sir."

"If anything like this happens in the future, you *will* report it to your commanding officer, not take it into your own hands. Is *that* understood?"

Johnny lowered his head. "Yes, sir. I recognize my mistake sir, and I apologize."

"The apologies need to go to your fellow Marine, not me. Now get out of here and enjoy the weekend."

Johnny snapped a salute. "Sir, yes sir. Thank you, sir."

After four weeks of training in various exercises, Sergeant Black-wood pulled Johnny aside one afternoon. "Private, I want you to focus on improving all skills the next couple of weeks, and I mean *all* of them. Field basics, marksmanship, and mental and visual acuity. I don't expect to see you falter at *any* of these. Is that understood, Private?"

"Sergeant, it is understood. Have I been lacking in any one area?"

Blackwood relaxed. "No, but I want you sharp because the brass have pegged you as a candidate for sniper school, and that's something you don't want to miss out on. But you've got to be sharp to be selected. And I don't just mean your shooting. Your shooting is plenty good. I haven't seen better, but you need to be able to handle the other parts of being a sniper—sitting still for days, being able to be a spotter as well as a shooter, being able to make spur-of-the-moment decisions that will determine a person's life. There are a lot more factors, and they all matter as much as the shooting."

Johnny grinned. It was everything he wanted. "I'll be prepared, Sergeant. Count on it."

Two more weeks passed and Johnny hadn't heard anything. He was getting nervous. Sergeant Blackwood must have known, or at least suspected, because he approached one day after training. "You're doing good, McCoy. Keep it up."

What he said gave Johnny all the inspiration he needed. He dove into his work with a newfound zeal, even to the point of doing exercises at night after a full day of training.

"Hey, McCoy, cut the shit. Some of us are trying to sleep," one of his bunkmates hollered one night.

"Yeah, I'm not gonna lose sleep because some ass like you wants to torture himself. If things are that bad, and you need to flog yourself, get a whip or a leather strap from Blackwood, then go outside and have at it. Just make sure you're quiet."

With four weeks of training to go, Johnny got promoted to Private First Class. As Blackwood bestowed the honors, he whispered to him. "Keep it up and Lance Corporal is right around the corner. You need to be Lance Corporal to qualify for sniper school."

"Thanks, Sergeant. This is what I've dreamed of."

"Just don't fuck up, Private. I don't like to recommend people who fuck up."

"If you don't mind me asking, Sergeant, and if it isn't too presumptuous, where is sniper school?"

"Quantico, VA, Private. And it'll be so grueling, you'll think you're back in Basic. Only about half the qualified Marines make it through."

"Half?" Johnny asked.

"Half. And half of them are only because they need snipers, so they end up accepting people they shouldn't. At least, that's what I'm told."

Johnny seemed perplexed. "Sergeant, how is that possible? If they select only the best marksmen, how can half of them fail?"

"Because, it's like I told you already, Private. Marksmanship is important, but it's only one piece of the pie. Hell, even if you make it, you might not be called on to shoot for years. Maybe never."

"What would I be doing then?"

"Be a spotter. Most snipers work in teams. A shooter and a spotter. Usually a team has one person better at shooting and one better at spotting, so that's how the assignment will be dished out. Most sniping is reconnaissance, not shooting. Snipers need to be able to sneak into a territory, get eyes on the enemy target or position, then gather data and report back to command. And they need to do this without being observed."

Johnny nodded. "I didn't realize that."

Sergeant Blackwood nodded. "If you want to be a shooter, be the best you can be, but that doesn't mean to neglect anything else. You've got to be able to do either job at any time to succeed."

"Thanks, Sergeant. I appreciate it."

"No problem, Private. Keep it up and be prepared to go to Quantico. That's my guess."

Sergeant Blackwood's guess turned out to be right. Johnny got his promotion to Lance Corporal, and he was given the opportunity to try out for sniper school at Quantico. As he packed his things to leave, Moj and Danny wished him well.

"You better do us proud, Private," Danny said. "I may be counting on you to save my ass someday."

"Yeah," Moj said. "I don't want to be telling people that I know the sniper who's got our backs and then have one of them get killed."

"Where are you guys going?" I asked. "Do you know where you'll be deployed yet?"

Danny shook his head. "Not yet. I guess it doesn't make much difference though."

"You won't think that if they send you someplace where they're shooting at your ass," Moj said.

"We don't have any armed conflicts going on," Danny said.

"Yeah, well give it a couple of months," Moj said. "They'll find someplace to get involved, and we'll be sent in to fix it."

Johnny slapped both of them on the back and wished them well. "Write to me once you get settled in," he said. "You can definitely reach me at Quantico, so let me know where you are."

"*If* you don't wash out," Moj said.

"I'm not about to wash out. I got this nailed."

Danny laughed. "I know you do, Johnny. Go get 'em. Give 'em hell."

Johnny finished saying his goodbyes, then he got on a bus bound for Cleveland, or at least one of the stops was going to be Cleveland. He was awarded seven days of leave before reporting to Quantico, and he intended to make the most of it.

Before leaving, he thought about calling Liz, but an announcement that the bus was about to leave forced him to forget that and hurry and grab a seat. If he was fortunate, he'd get one near the back where he could rest—assuming he didn't have a seat companion.

As the bus pulled away from Camp Lejeune, Johnny breathed a sigh of relief—he had no one sitting next to him. He kicked up his feet and stretched out as much as he could, lay his head on his knapsack, and closed his eyes. *Ready or not, here I come, Liz.*

WELCOME HOME

LATE SUMMER, 2001

Johnny got off the bus and caught a ride to Dom and Clorinda's house. He opened the front door quietly and walked inside. Tony was just coming down the stairs, but Johnny hushed him before he said anything. "Where's Aunt Clorinda?" he whispered.

Tony pointed to the kitchen, and he and Johnny both tiptoed in. Aunt Clorinda stood with her back to them, doing dishes. Johnny walked up behind her and tapped her on the shoulder. "Need any help, older lady?"

Aunt Clorinda spun around and gasped, then she laughed and pulled Johnny close to hug. "Look at you!" she said. "*Look* at you. So darn big." She squeezed his biceps several times. "And muscular too."

"How did you get home? And why did they let you out?"

Tony laughed. "Mom, give Johnny a minute to breathe. Besides, I'm sure Dad's gonna have the same questions when he gets home. We ought to wait till then."

Clorinda nodded. "All right. All right. But we at least need something special for dinner. Tony, how about you go to Rubino's and pick up some ravioli? And take Johnny with you—if he *wants* to go. In the meantime, I'll get started on meatballs and sauce."

"I'm all for that," Tony said. "How much ravioli you want?"

"You better get two pounds. That way, we'll have leftovers. Johnny loves leftovers."

Johnny leaned down and kissed her. "Aunt Clorinda, I love everything you cook. It's all good." He laughed hard. "And when you compare it to what we get in the service, it's *fantastico*."

Johnny rode with Tony to the market, and they chatted the whole way. "So fill me in," Tony said. "What's going on? What have they got you doing?"

Johnny grinned. "Don't say anything yet 'cause I want to be the one to tell Uncle Dom, but they're sending me to sniper school."

Tony's voice was so loud it sounded as if he was shouting. "What? Are you shitting me? Sniper school? You know how hard it is to get in there? Damn, my cousin is going to be a sniper."

"Whoa," Johnny said. "They invited me to go to school. That doesn't mean I'll make the cut. It's like being invited to try out for the Cavaliers or the Browns. Trying out doesn't mean you make the team."

"I'm not worried about that," Tony said. "You'll make it. I have no doubt."

"I hope so, Tony. But thanks for the vote of confidence. I'm gonna need it."

Johnny and Tony picked up the ravioli and headed for home. Ronnie was there when they arrived. He raced out the door and hugged Johnny. "You son of a bitch. You didn't even tell us you were coming."

"I didn't get much notice, Ronnie. They issued my new assignment, then said I had seven days leave. I had to pack and catch the bus or risk being stuck at Camp Lejeune. And believe me, I didn't want any part of that. It wasn't boot camp, but it wasn't much better."

"Where are you going? Where did they assign you?"

"I'll tell you tonight when I tell your dad," Johnny said.

Dom walked in the front door. He wasn't dragging his feet, but the expression on his face looked as if he were.

"Tough day, honey?" Clorinda asked.

"More than tough. I may be getting too old for this. Maybe it's time we thought about retirement."

"You're right about getting too old," Johnny yelled from a side of the kitchen, where he couldn't be seen.

"And you can go to hell, Tony," Dom said. "I'm not so old I can't kick your ass."

Johnny stepped out in front of Dom. "How about mine, old man? I'm not Tony."

Dom backed up a step and stared. "Johnny! What the heck are you doing here?" Dom embraced him and hugged. "You son of a gun. It's good to see you."

Clorinda put plates filled with steaming ravioli and meatballs on the table. "Come and sit down. We can talk while we eat."

Johnny ate like he hadn't had a meal in days, shoveling ravioli into his mouth while barely breathing.

Aunt Clorinda laughed. "I had Tony pick up two pounds thinking we'd have plenty of leftovers, but I don't think we will. I think Johnny's going to eat it all by himself."

Johnny put his fork down. "Sorry, Aunt Clorinda, I didn't—"

She waved her hand in the air. "Nonsense. I was only kidding. I'm thrilled to see you eat so much. If you hadn't, I would have been worried."

"So tell us what's going on, Johnny. Are you finished with training now?"

Johnny nodded while he swallowed, then he said. "I got promoted to Lance Corporal, Uncle Dom, and they invited me to go to sniper school."

"What? Where?"

"Quantico, VA," Johnny said. "I report in one week."

"How long is training?" Tony asked.

"Ten weeks, but the dropout rate is high. Really high."

Johnny and the rest of the family chatted all through dinner, and when they were done, they retired to the living room. "Look at this," Aunt Clorinda said. "We even have enough for tomorrow night."

"I won't be here tomorrow night," Johnny said. "I have a date."

"A date?" Uncle Dom asked. "Who is it? Do we know her?"

"No way you know her," Ronnie said. "We don't even know her."

"You need to bring her by," Aunt Clorinda said. "She needs to taste my pasta. If she doesn't like my sauce, you might have a problem."

Johnny laughed. "Not to worry," Johnny said. "She likes Amatuzio's sauce, and that's the closest I've tasted to yours, so I think we're good."

Johnny surprised Liz the next night by making reservations at Mia Bella's in Little Italy. He knew she loved the food there.

As usual, Liz ordered the seafood ravioli, though it wasn't their signature dish. She loved it though, and swore by it, proclaiming it the best in town.

Johnny and Liz had been there enough that the waiters knew them by name, although he addressed them by their Italian names. Johnny entered with Liz accompanying him, and they were greeted by Antonio.

"Ciao, Gianni and Elisabetta. *Benvenuti nella nostra cucina.*"

Antonio handed them menus and left. Liz leaned over to Johnny. "Do you know what he said?" she asked.

Johnny laughed. "He said, 'welcome to our kitchen.' That's all. A standard greeting at Italian restaurants."

"Speaking of which," Liz said, "when am I going to meet your family? I've heard all about them, but I've never met them. Are you embarrassed of me? Is it because I'm black?"

"God, no." Johnny said. "I didn't realize you wanted to meet them. I'll make it happen, and soon. Before I go back to the Marines."

THE SURPRISE

Johnny worried all week about how to tell Uncle Dom and Aunt Clorinda about Liz. He wasn't embarrassed about her, not at all, but he did worry about what they'd think. After all, interracial dating wasn't common in their day. He didn't know how they'd feel.

While Johnny worried, he continued going out with Liz, taking her to eat, going to the movies, to plays, and his favorite—walks in the park. They usually went to the park late at night, when few people were there. One night, after a particularly late walk, Brandon met them at the front door when Johnny brought Liz home.

"Were you ever going to come by and see me?" he asked. "Or is it all about my cousin, Liz, now?"

Johnny laughed. "If I said it wasn't about her, I'd be lying, and I think you already know that. You'd have to get a lot prettier than you are to compete, Brandon."

He laughed. "Screw you, McCoy. Have you at least been watching out for her?"

"If you mean 'watching out' as in checking on the serial killer, yes. But I thought he was gone. Didn't they catch him?"

Brandon shook his head. "Not that I know of, but then again, who can believe what the cops tell you. There haven't been any recent killings, but I haven't heard of any arrests either."

"So it could be that the killer is just taking a break and will start it up again soon?"

"Unlikely, but yeah, it could be. A better guess would be he moved on to another city, but we may never know."

"We'll find out," Johnny said. "Don't worry about that. I'm gonna get Uncle Dom to look in on it. His buddies too. One of them will find something."

"All right, Johnny. In the meantime, it's up to you to protect my cousin. Agreed?"

Johnny laughed. "Agreed. And I'll make sure she gets home by midnight too."

Brandon smiled at that one, then I leaned over and kissed Liz goodnight. "See you tomorrow," Johnny said. "And make sure to dress up because I'll have a surprise for you."

Johnny slept on the sofa in the living room, but *slept* didn't properly describe what he did. Most of the night, he rolled over, sat up and made notes, or went to the kitchen to get a drink of water. And he knew what brought this on. He was worried sick about introducing Liz to Aunt Clorinda and Uncle Dom.

He didn't even know if he had anything to worry about. He'd never heard them say anything derogatory about black people—not about *any* people for that matter. And he had no reason to believe they'd care from anything Tony or Ronnie said either. Still, it bothered him. He grew up in a house where bringing home a black person as a girlfriend would have been worse than murder. Hell, his father beat him senseless for just playing ball with some black kids.

After he gulped down another glass of water and took a trip to relieve himself of it, he sat on the sofa and pondered. Finally, he decided that he'd do it tonight. He didn't have time to waste.

And if I'm gonna bring her here tonight, I've got to tell Aunt Clorinda and Uncle Dom this morning.

The breakfast table was filled with chatter about upcoming events and general chit-chat—all except Johnny. He sat at the end of the table quietly eating; in fact, not saying a word.

"You're awfully quiet," Aunt Clorinda said. "Anything wrong, Johnny?"

"Yeah, it's not like you to sit so long and not run your mouth about *something*," Tony said. "And it's usually something you know nothing about."

"*Usually?*" Ronnie asked.

"All right. All right," Johnny said. He put his utensils down and placed his hands on the table. "I don't know how to say this, so I guess I'll just come right out and say it."

"Oh, shit. Are you gay?" Ronnie asked.

Ronnie got Johnny laughing. "No, asshole. I'm *not* gay, but I hope what I'm going to tell you guys will be accepted the same way that kind of news should be."

"Spit it out," Tony said. "I want to finish eating."

"Liz, my girlfriend, is black."

Uncle Dom's face took on a grim expression. He set his fork beside his plate and looked at Johnny. "Is she black *and* gay? Or just black?"

At that, everyone laughed, even Aunt Clorinda. "Dom, you're cruel," she said.

Uncle Dom reached over and patted Johnny's hand. "Johnny, this isn't your old house, and I'm not your old man. I don't give a damn what color Liz is. If you like her, you like her. That's all that matters. And I know your aunt feels the same way."

"Really? Uncle Dom, that's great. I was afraid to tell you guys."

"Don't ever be afraid to tell us anything," Dom said. "I always told your mother—God rest her soul—that Michael's attitude and opinion about blacks and Asians, and damn near everyone else, was racist. She agreed, but she'd never do anything about it because of the church's stance on divorced people."

"I thought that changed," Johnny said.

"It did, but your mother was old school, and divorce was taboo. Even if one of the partners was suffering. And God only knows, she suffered."

Johnny dived into his plate with relish. "I can't tell you guys how good this makes me feel. I was so worried, I couldn't sleep last night."

Aunt Clorinda stood and began clearing the table, taking the plates from Ronnie and Tony. "What you should do is bring her over for dinner, Johnny. She's got to have concerns, and she needs to see that we don't care about her being black."

Johnny stopped eating, got up, and hugged his aunt. "You made me day, Aunt Clorinda. When can we do that? I don't have a lot of time."

"As soon as you can convince one of your brothers to go to Rubino's and get ravioli and some stuffed mushrooms." She turned to Ronnie, her eyebrows raised. "Ronnie, can you go?"

"Johnny, I hope you know this is messing with my championship games at the arcade."

Johnny laughed. "Ronnie, it's long past time you quit going to that arcade. People already think you're a narc just hanging out there to bust people."

"Oh, and get regular mushrooms, Ronnie. And ask Rita if she has any of her Gorgonzola sauce."

Aunt Clorinda was already in a frenzy, figuring out what had to be gotten and what needed to be done. "Johnny, we can do it tonight if that's all right?"

"Fantastic," Johnny said, and kissed her cheek.

"Johnny, it's silly of me, but I forgot to ask. Does Liz like Italian food? And does she like stuffed mushrooms?"

"Yes and yes," Johnny said as he raced upstairs.

Ronnie hollered as he took the steps two at a time. "Oh, and don't worry, Johnny, your nice brother Ronnie will pick up the food."

"Thanks, Ronnie," Johnny hollered back. "Sorry, but I've got to change and get going. I've got a few things to do before I pick Liz up. Aunt Clorinda, is seven o'clock okay?"

"That's perfect, Johnny. I'll have dinner ready. But you make sure you find some time between now and then to stop by and help clean up."

"Will do, Aunt Clorinda. See ya."

THE DINNER

Johnny picked up Liz at the usual time, and as he asked, she had dressed up. She looked gorgeous. He gave a low whistle when she answered the door. "Damn, you look good," he said.

"Good enough to eat?" she asked.

"No question about that," Johnny said, "but that may have to wait till later. I've got reservations."

"Ooh," Liz said. "I like the sound of that; in fact, I like the sound of both things you said—the later part *and* the reservations. Where are we going?"

"None of your business," Johnny said. "But I promise you won't have better food."

"Now I like it even more," she said, and grabbed his arm. "Lead the way."

Johnny drove for about fifteen minutes and Liz said nothing about the direction, but when he turned off the interstate leading into the city, Liz looked around and then asked him. "Is this a new place? I didn't know of any good Italian restaurants out this way."

"It's definitely a new place. A good one too. Dom and Clorinda's Cucina Italiana."

"Dom and Clorinda's? Aren't they your aunt and uncle's names?"

Johnny smiled. "They are, my love. And Aunt Clorinda is cooking something special just for you."

"What? Oh, my God." Liz panicked. "Johnny, I can't meet them looking like this."

"Looking like what? You're gorgeous."

"Gorgeous? My hair is too frizzy, my dress is too short, and—oh, God, I'm not wearing makeup. Johnny, you've got to take me back."

Johnny laughed. "Don't be ridiculous. No one will care about any of that. My aunt and uncle aren't the kind of people that care about those things."

Liz got sheepish. "What about . . .?"

"About you being black?" Johnny asked. "I already told them, and they didn't think twice about it. And as far as turning back, it's not going to happen. When Aunt Clorinda puts her food on the table, she expects people to be there and ready to eat."

Liz looked at Johnny and shook her head. "All right, mister. If you say so."

"I say so," Johnny said.

"What is she cooking? Am I going to have to pretend to like it?"

"Not a chance. You're gonna love it. I don't know for certain, but I think there will be stuffed mushrooms to start with, and they'll be followed by the best ravioli you've ever eaten. It's stuffed with diced chicken and crabmeat, then covered with a Gorgonzola sauce and mushrooms. I'm getting hungry talking about it."

"I'm past that. The stuffed mushrooms did it for me. The rest of what you described is pure heaven."

Johnny and Liz walked in the front door at six forty-five, plenty of time for introductions before dinner. Clorinda raced over and embraced Liz, giving her a big hug and a kiss on the cheek. "I'm glad you could come for dinner, Liz. It's so nice to meet you." Clorinda turned and headed toward the kitchen. "Make yourself at home while I finish dinner. And don't mind the mess. I asked the boys to help clean, but I'm sure you know how that goes—vacuum and dust only what you can see and leave the rest alone."

Liz laughed. "Yes, ma'am. I have brothers too."

"And cut out the ma'am. You make me feel old. It's just Clorinda, and my husband is Dom. He should be down at any minute. At least, he *better* be down."

Liz squeezed Johnny's hand and smiled, then she whispered in his ear. "I love her. She's so sweet."

During dinner, they talked about a lot of things, though most of the topics centered around food. "Oh, good Lord, this is good," Liz said. "I *love* Gorgonzola sauce, but I've never had any this good."

"I'd like to take credit," Clorinda said. "But I got it at Rubino's. Rita Petrucci has been making it for twenty years, and it's always good. I don't even try it myself. Hers is too good."

"Hey, Uncle Dom, what have you heard about a serial killer preying on young black girls in the city? Liz's cousin told me about it. Anything to it?"

Dom finished chewing, and then nodded. "Yes and no. We definitely had a problem a while ago, but then it went away. The killings just stopped. Some people speculated it may have been someone who got put in prison for something else, so they're not on the streets anymore. Others say whoever it was died. And others still say the guy packed up and moved to another city. I don't know which of those or a hundred other theories are right, but I'm damn glad he's gone. Life is tough enough without having to protect your kids from some dam lunatic."

"So, you think people are safe now?" Johnny asked.

"I didn't say that," Dom said. "Hell, people are never safe. You've always gotta be on the lookout for some kind of crazy 'cause sure as shit as soon as you let your guard down, something will happen."

"That's not what he's asking, Dom," Aunt Clorinda said. "And stop with your nonsense. You'll scare Liz to death."

"Well, he asked," Dom said.

"No, he asked specifically about that serial killer. Nothing else. You were giving him a history of crime in the city."

Johnny dabbed his face with a napkin, but it was really a guise to hide his smile. Aunt Clorinda had him pegged just right. She knew Uncle Dom better than he knew himself.

A moment later, Liz finished with her plate and picked it up to carry to the sink. "That was more than delicious," she said. "Johnny told me I wouldn't have better food, and I think he's right."

Clorinda stood and waved her hand. "Nonsense, but thank you." She grabbed the plate from Liz and placed it in the sink. "Now sit back down. I've got some cannoli for dessert. And, of course, coffee."

Liz and Johnny sat at the table and talked for hours. Even Ronnie and Tony stayed for more than an hour. Finally, Liz looked at the time and said, "It's almost ten, Johnny. I've got to get going. I have to get up early."

Johnny took the coffee cups and dessert plates to the sink, kissed Aunt Clorinda on the cheek, and shook Uncle Dom's hand. "Thanks so much, guys. This was fantastic."

Liz looked as if she didn't know what to do, then Dom leaned over and kissed her cheek. "It was so nice to meet you, Liz. Just make sure you take care of this big brat. Goodness knows, he's a handful."

"I'll bet he is," Liz said, then she and Johnny left.

"I can't believe how nice they were," Liz said as they pulled away from the house. "They were the nicest white people I've ever met."

Johnny laughed. "Then you just haven't met enough white people. Come to think of it, that's the problem on both sides. Black people only meet the racist whites, and whites only meet the blacks who cause trouble. If the normal people got to know each other, it would be totally different."

For the remainder of his stay, Johnny and Liz were almost inseparable. They went out *every* night for walks or to a show or to dinner. Some nights, they did all three.

Johnny parked the car and walked Liz to the door. After she unlocked it, he turned her around and kissed her goodnight—a long kiss.

"You're going to spoil me if you keep this up."

"Keep what up?" Johnny asked.

"The attention, and loving, and fine dining. All of it."

"Well, I hate to break it to you, but I intend to keep that up for about forty or fifty years, so get used to it. It's not going to stop."

Liz smiled ear-to-ear. "I think I could get used to that, Johnny McCoy. But beware, you may be creating a monster."

"I can handle monsters," Johnny said. "What I can't handle are jealous women."

Liz kissed him again. "Don't give me any reason for jealousy, and I'll never be jealous. I promise."

Johnny held her by the shoulders and pulled her close. "You know, I've gotta report to Quantico in two days, which means we only have one night left."

"Which means we should stay at the Marriott tonight. Don't you think?"

"Are you sure?" Johnny asked. "It's a big step."

Liz grabbed Johnny's hand and headed back out. "I've got long legs, so big steps are easy."

Johnny laughed. "And yet another reason why I love you," he said.

Liz looked up at Johnny. "Do you? Do you really love me?"

Johnny stopped, pulled Liz to him, and said, "You bet your sweet ass, I do."

"Ooh, my sweet ass, huh? How do you know it's sweet?"

"I don't yet, but I intend to find out soon. Tonight, in fact."

"Then we better hurry," Liz said. "I like it when someone enjoys my sweet ass. And by the way, sweet it is."

Johnny and Liz checked into the Marriott, had a few drinks, then retired to the room. "I'm going to take a shower, but I won't be long."

"You need someone to wash your back?" Johnny asked.

"In fact, I might," Liz said. "At least, my backside. Step in the shower and show me what you can do."

Liz and Johnny made love all night, had an early breakfast, then continued the lovemaking. Finally, after complete exhaustion, they lay on the bed, laughing. "I didn't think it was possible to make love so much," Liz said.

"It's not," Johnny said. "I think we just set a world's record."

"What do we do now?" Liz asked. "Do I come with you when you go back?"

"Not yet," Johnny said. "Let me finish sniper school, then you can join me, no matter where I go. If you want to, that is."

"Of course, I want to. As long as I'm allowed, I'll be with you."

Johnny wrapped his arms around her and kissed her. "They can't stop you if you're my wife."

"Your wife? Johnny are you . . .?"

"Yes, I think I am. So what do you say? I don't have a ring to offer, but I'll get one."

"Yes. Yes. Yes. Of course, yes."

"Good, when I'm done with Quantico, we'll make plans and set a date."

"I'll be waiting," Liz said. "And I'll be thinking about you every day."

"Keep writing those great letters. And write a lot. I read them every night. I'll be done in a few months, so it won't be long."

QUANTICO

FALL, 2011, QUANTICO, VA

Sniper school was a surprise for Johnny. Despite what Blackwood had told him, he'd expected it to be easy, a piece of cake. But much like Blackwood warned, the shooting was only a small part of what he had to endure. The worst was probably the patience and the endurance testing.

At one point, during week five, he and his teammate had to simulate a deep, deep cover where even the slightest movement was out of the question.

They wore ghillie suits, which are a type of camouflage clothing designed to look like whatever background environment the person is in, such as foliage, snow or sand. Sometimes, the suit is made more realistic by adding leaves and twigs and leaves.

It was so bad, they had to be catheterized and pee in a bag so they didn't have to get up to pee. They remained in a lying position for almost two days straight until they gathered the information they needed.

Johnny's partner was a guy named Fritz from Boston. When they finally got word to break cover, they sneaked away without making a sound.

"All that shit, and we didn't even kill anyone?" Fritz said. "Seems like a waste of time."

"I'm with you, Fritz, but the brass said sometimes it's better to gather data than it is to kill someone. I don't see it, but what the hell, orders are orders."

"Guess so," Fritz said. "I just know I can't wait to take a shower. You need one too, McCoy. You stink."

Johnny laughed. "I don't think they'd let either one of us in the barracks before we showered."

Every night, Johnny relaxed while he read the letters from Liz, and she wrote almost every day, so he had lots to read. As he lay in bed, reading yet another one, Fritz walked by.

"Still reading that bullshit from your girlfriend?" he asked. "You know she's probably writing them while some other dude is humping her, don't you?"

"Fritz, not everyone is as cynical as you, so no, I don't *know* that, and I don't believe that."

"You think you're the exception?" Fritz asked.

Johnny laughed. "No, Fritz, I think *you're* the exception. Not everyone is a low-life who can't be trusted."

For two more weeks, Johnny and Fritz endured hell, either put into positions where they couldn't move or placed in situations where they had to pretend to be locals and 'fit in' with the rest of the crowd. Johnny could do that in some of the modern European countries, but in the Middle East, he found it difficult. He found it difficult to pronounce the words properly. Fritz, on the other hand, was stellar at it. He spoke five languages fluently, and it took him little time to learn enough of the language to get by on. He was a great partner to have.

By week nine, the commanding officer informed them they were near the top in performance, and if they kept up the good work, they may well finish in the top three. Johnny took a shower, ate a huge dinner, then settled in for the night, intent on reading his mail. He had a big stack of unread letters, so he plopped on the bed and set the letters on his lap, ready to be opened.

The first one was from Ronnie and Tony. He laughed as he opened it. The letters were always addressed as being from both of them. Johnny suspected Ronnie did the writing though because Tony wasn't much on writing. The other *big* clue was that the letters always contained reports of any new high scores on games at the arcade, and the games mentioned were the ones Ronnie was fond of.

Aunt Clorinda and Uncle Dom each sent a letter, as did Aunt Trudy. Disappointment set in when he didn't see one from Liz. He checked to make sure he had all the mail and afterward opened the remaining letter—one from Brandon. He unsealed the envelope and leaned back to read, but the first sentence sent him reeling.

'Johnny, I don't know how to say this, so I'll just say it. Liz is dead.'

After Johnny recovered enough, he continued reading.

She was walking across the parking lot from her workplace to her car when someone shot her. The police are saying it's the same serial killer who shot the other young black women. I thought the city had rid itself of him because we hadn't heard anything about new victims. I can see now, the sick son of a bitch was here all along. We just didn't hear about it.

We are all devastated, as I'm sure you are. She'll be buried on Friday. I hope you can get here somehow.

Johnny put his head in his hands and cried. He thought back to his mother being killed, and that made him cry more. He thought he'd been over that, but now he guessed he never would be. He found the strength to stand, then he turned and punched the wall several times. The third one made a hole in the wall.

The news from Brandon sapped his strength—even his will to go on, but vengeance instilled a new resolve. One that drove him even harder. He balled his hands into fists and squeezed. *I'll find the son of a bitch who did this. And when I do, I'll put a bullet through his brain.*

When he checked the date on the letter, it showed that Liz was already buried, so he didn't even get to see her before she went in the ground. Truth be told though, he didn't know if he wanted to. It might be better to have only the memories of her alive and vibrant.

If Liz's death wasn't enough, the next day brought news of a terrorist attack on the World Trade Center and the Pentagon. Every Marine in the camp was fired up, but Johnny seemed to be affected more so.

For the remaining time in school, Johnny used his newly instilled resolve to push him harder than ever, harder even than the commanding officers demanded. If they asked for five kilometers, he gave them six or seven. No matter what they asked, he did more. By the end of school, he was in the best shape of his life, and his marksmanship ranked second only to one man—a Marine from Texas who said he'd been shooting since he was three. Ordinarily, Johnny may have found that difficult to believe, but the man's targets told the tale.

After graduation from sniper school, Johnny expected action. He looked forward to it. What he got were boring assignments in places he didn't much care for. His first deployment was Lebanon, where the fighting seemed to be endless. Unfortunately, Johnny expected to use his marksmanship on assignment, but everything was reconnaissance. Even if shooting had been required, Johnny wouldn't have been the one to do it. He was the designated spotter, not the shooter. The assignments in Lebanon usually involved reporting the movement of enemy troops and were often conducted from rooftops near the edge of the border. After almost six months of continual work, he was finally given an assignment that showed promise—Afghanistan. He'd be doing something that would affect the sons of bitches who attacked his country.

His first few assignments featured him as the spotter, but after that, he received his first kill mission. It was a highly sought after fugitive, and Johnny had to wait three days before he got a shot at him. There were several times when he felt he couldn't sit still another moment, but when that happened, he thought about Liz, and he remembered Brandon's words: *Johnny, I don't know how to say this, so I'll just say it. Liz is dead.*

Most of all, he remembered how he had felt like dying himself. He was crushed, devastated, heartbroken. And he swore he'd get the son of a bitch who did that to her. Once again, he made a vow that he'd do it. He didn't know exactly how or when, but he'd get him.

He was able to be still after that. Motionless even. And he only had to wait a short while longer. When he took the shot, it was as Blackwood had told him—a mixed bag. Johnny felt bad because the man's family was there, but on the other hand, the man was a terrorist who had killed innocent Americans.

Johnny took aim and fired the shot. It only took one, going along with the motto that many snipers had taken to heart—*One shot. One kill.*

Johnny ended up registering thirty-seven confirmed kills in Afghanistan during the next two years. That included zero missed targets. As a result, three years after graduating sniper school, he was promoted to sergeant and told he was going home—not quite *home*, as in Cleveland, but he *was* going to the US. It seemed as if former DI Benz, from Parris Island, had transferred to Camp Pendleton and he was close friends with the colonel. At Benz's suggestion, the colonel requested McCoy to help train recruits how to shoot.

BACK IN THE USA

SUMMER, 2005 CAMP PENDLETON, SOUTHERN CALIFORNIA

Johnny showed up on a Friday afternoon and reported to the colonel. "Colonel, sir. I'm Johnny McCoy. You asked me to report here?"

"At ease, Sergeant. Yes, Benz spoke highly of you; in fact, he boldly stated he'd never seen a better shot."

Johnny tried not to smile, but he felt sure at least a grin escaped. "Thank you, sir. DI Benz was an excellent mentor. Is it still DI or has he been promoted?"

"No, he's still DI. I think he always will be. He loves it. And he's damn good at it." The colonel walked around his desk and pointed to the expanse that was Camp Pendleton. "What we've got here, McCoy is a great Marine base with too many distractions. We've got the ocean, the mountains, and we've got LA not far to the north and San Diego not far to the south. All those are opportunities for Marines to distract themselves from what needs to be done."

"And how do you think I can help, sir?"

"You can show them what a real sniper can do. You can train them to shoot better so they are driven to become experts with the rifle. If you do that, maybe a few more of them will put in the extra time necessary to become better than just *good.*"

Johnny snapped a salute. "I'll do my best, sir. If someone can show me to my bunk, I'll get ready."

Colonel Rogers got on the intercom. "Bennett, tell him to come in. McCoy is ready to retire."

A moment later, DI Benz walked in. He laughed and slapped Johnny on the back. "Whoa! I see it's *Sergeant McCoy* now."

Johnny laughed and hugged Benz. "Good to see you. It's been a long time. Seems like forever."

Benz grabbed hold of his elbow and led him toward the door. "C'mon. I'll take you to a local hangout, and you can buy *me* a beer."

"Lead the way," Johnny said.

Johnny and Benz had a few beers, and Benz filled him in on his problems. "A lot of the recruits here become infatuated with so much to do close by. It's not like what we had on Parris Island or even what you had at Camp Lejeune. Neither one of those places was a paradise of fun activity or things to do. Here, it's different. LA, San Diego, the mountains, the beach . . . There's too much for them to look forward to when free time comes, so instead of focusing on what they need to do to improve their shooting, they're thinking of what they need to do to pick up a chick they met last week."

"And you think making them better marksmen will help?"

"I don't know if it will, but either way, it'll be good. It can't hurt."

"I'm fine with whatever you want, DI. I'm just happy to be close to home."

Benz cocked his head and stared. "Close to home? Aren't you from Cleveland?"

Johnny laughed. "I am, but I've been overseas for going on three years, so while LA isn't *close*, it *is* a lot closer."

"Where overseas you talking about?" Benz asked. "If you can say."

"Lebanon and Afghanistan mostly. At first, it was all reconnaissance, but that changed when we got to Afghanistan."

"Either assignment is good. Reconnaissance or sniping. You know what they say. A bullet kills one, but a good pair of eyes can save hundreds."

"Well, I must have saved thousands because I watched so much shit in Lebanon, I think I wore my eyes out."

Benz and Johnny chatted for about fifteen more minutes, then a tall blond-haired woman dragged a chair across the floor in their direction. Johnny jumped up and offered to help. "May I take this for you, ma'am?"

"Thank goodness. Yes, you can."

Johnny picked up the chair effortlessly, though it was quite heavy. It wasn't a standard bar chair that you ordinarily see, but a thick, heavy oaken chair. "Where would you like me to set it, ma'am?"

She glanced around, then gestured to Johnny's table. "I guess right there would be fine."

Johnny looked confused. "Pardon me, ma'am. *That* table? Do you know DI Benz?"

She smiled broadly. "I do now. Thanks for the introduction." She then held out her hand. "And by the way, my name's Michele—with one 'l' in Michele. What's yours?"

Johnny was thrown completely off by the effrontery of this woman. "Ma'am, do I know you?"

"For the love of God, Marine, I just introduced myself. Do I need to do it again."

Benz laughed until his sides hurt. "Welcome to California, McCoy. Nothing's like it was back east. Out here, the women are as forward as the men, so you better get used to it." Benz took the chair from Johnny and set it between them. "Have a seat, Michele with one 'l.'"

As she sat down, Benz pushed his chair in and took his leave. "I'm gonna leave this with you, McCoy. I've got to get home to my wife." He smiled as he walked away.

Johnny said, "All right, Benz. Have a good weekend. I'll see you on Monday." He then picked up his mug and moved to the bar, taking the stool near the end.

Michele shook her head, then looked left and right. She signaled a waitress, who came by immediately.

"We're moving to the bar. Get me whatever is on tap, and bring him another of what he's drinking, please. And put it on my tab," she said as the waitress walked away.

Michele sat on the stool next to Johnny and smiled. "You didn't think you'd get rid of me so quickly, did you? Give me some credit. I'm a little more persistent than that."

"Thanks for the drink," Johnny said, "but I could have gotten my own; besides, I usually don't take drinks from women."

"Really? Do you have to turn them down often, soldier?"

136

"It's not *soldier*, ma'am. It's—"

Michele laughed. "I know, it's *Marine.* I just wanted to see how far up your ass your head was stuck. Seems like it's a good ways up there."

Despite everything, Johnny had to laugh. "You're a character," he said.

"Right out of a Hollywood movie," she said.

Johnny decided on something right then. He closed his eyes, then turned his head toward Michele. "Listen, I appreciate the drink, and I appreciate all you've said and done, but you might want to find someone else to chat with."

"Why is that?"

"Because I don't think I'd be good company. Not now."

"Why not? You don't like women?"

Johnny laughed. "No, it's not that, it's just . . ."

"Just what? You don't like *me*? Do I rub you the wrong way? Do you not like forward, aggressive women?"

Johnny swiveled the barstool around so he faced her and stared. "I just lost my girlfriend. She was killed by a serial killer, so I'm not up for another relationship right now. In fact, I'm not up for much of anything right now. Is that enough to satisfy you? Or do you need more?"

"Oh, my God," Michele said, the shock evident. "I'm so sorry. I had no idea." She then excused herself and sat at a table in the corner of the bar.

Johnny watched her sit down, and he felt bad—as if he'd chased her away, which is what he actually did. He grabbed his beer, walked to the table, and sat down. "Excuse me for being an ass. I can get mopey when something like this happens."

"I hope something like this doesn't happen to you all that much," she said.

Johnny lowered his head. "Unfortunately, it seems to. My mother was killed when I was eleven."

She gasped, her hands moving up to cover her mouth. "Oh, my God."

He nodded. "To make it worse, she was shot by my father, who then killed himself. Luckily, he did it all in front of me so I'd always remember it." Johnny shook his head. "And remember it, I do. Every damn night I remember it—in detail."

Johnny slugged the rest of his beer, looked at Michele, and said, "So that's why I'm reluctant. Everyone I've really cared about—not *everyone*—but several important ones, have ended up being killed. First, my mother and more recently, my girlfriend Liz."

Michele reached over and held Johnny's hand. "Tell me about Liz," she said. "What was she like?"

SOMEBODY NEW

Johnny hesitated. He'd never told anyone about Liz. Never talked about her being killed except with those who already knew. He stared at Michele, took a sip of his drink, then started.

"There's not a lot to tell, Michele. I met her through my best friend while I was home on leave from Basic—she was his cousin—and we fell for each other. Before I went to sniper school, I—"

"Whoa! You were at sniper school? Did you graduate?"

I nodded. "Second in class. And I've been overseas for three years."

"Sorry to interrupt," Michele said. "Go on."

"So before school, I got leave, and Liz and I spent every minute together. I asked her to marry me before going back. We planned on a wedding right after graduation."

Johnny paused for a long time, looking one way, then another. "It was while I was in school, she got killed. Shot down like a mad dog. No reason."

Michele took hold of his hands, which were rattling the silverware against the plates because he trembled so much. "I'm sorry, Johnny. I shouldn't have asked."

"It's not that," he said. "I've never told anybody before, and I got worked up telling it. I didn't think it would bother me so much, but it did."

"I'm sorry I was the cause of your discomfort," she said, then glanced at the clock hanging on the wall. "Oh, crap. I didn't know it was so late. Listen, Johnny, I've got to go, but let's do this. I'm not going to be pushy or nervy, but I'm going to give you my phone number." She rifled through her purse and pulled out a card, then handed it to him. "I'd like to see you again, and for real, not sitting in a bar. If you want the same, call that number. Sound good?"

Johnny looked at her, then nodded. "I'll think about it."

"All a girl can ask for," Michele said. "Goodnight." She leaned over and pecked his cheek, dropped a twenty on the table, then left.

Once she'd gone, Johnny ordered another beer and thought about what had happened. He didn't realize talking about it would tire him out so much, but it did. He then looked at the card he held in his hand:

Michele Arnold

Marketing Manager

Barnes and Gershwin

(213) 555-7799

He fidgeted with the card for a moment, then tucked it into his wallet. He didn't know if he'd call, but something about her made him want to. He liked her.

The week went as expected. Most of the men resented Johnny being there at first, but after they saw how he could shoot, their attitudes changed. Each day, Johnny worked with three or four men, usually the ones who needed help the most, and on Friday, he gave a teaching demonstration for the entire team.

When he got back to his bunk on Friday night, he pondered what to do, then decided to call Michele. He doubted she'd be available or even around to answer the phone, and as he thought about it, he wondered if that wasn't why he waited so long—hoping she wouldn't be available. After all, the number on her card was a work number, and it was already six o'clock on a Friday.

The phone rang five times with no answer. Johnny was about to hang up when a familiar voice said, "It's about time you called, soldier. I've been waiting on pins and needles all week."

Johnny felt relieved when he heard her voice. "Then let me make it up to you. How about dinner tonight?"

"Name the place, but be warned, I'm hungry."

"How about Jake's in Del Mar? DI Benz said it was excellent."

"I'm game," Michele said. "I've been there, and it is good. It's better than good. I'm in LA though, and you're in Pendleton. It would work better if either I picked you up or we met at the restaurant."

"How about we meet at the restaurant? Say eight?"

"Eight it is, but I'll be hungrier by then. Although on a Friday night, it will probably take that long to get there."

Johnny met Michele, and both were on time, pulling up within minutes of each other. They got a table, ordered a glass of wine and appetizers, then settled in for some deep conversation. Johnny took a sip of his wine and said, "You know . . . I don't know why I called you."

Michele laughed. "Wait, let me write that down because it may be the best pickup line I've ever heard. It makes me want to take you home and jump in bed with you."

Johnny laughed. "I'm sorry. I tend to do that—just say whatever comes to mind without thinking how it sounds."

"That's all right. I know exactly what you mean, and I'd probably do the same thing if I were in your shoes. You don't just forget things like what you experienced. Even after you move on—if you can move on—you don't forget. You never forget."

Johnny looked across the table at Michele. "You sound as if you really understand. Did something happen to you?"

"Nothing like you experienced, but I lost my little brother when he died in a swimming accident. He was twelve. I didn't witness it. I wasn't there. We weren't even particularly close. But he was my brother, and I miss him dearly."

"Sorry to hear," Johnny said. "Losing anyone is tough, but when a person goes so young, it's really tough."

"Well, enough dreariness," Michele said. "Tell me about yourself, and what you plan to do with your life. Or are you destined to be a lifer?"

"I'm not sure," Johnny said. "I've given thought to staying in the service, but I'm not positive. Not yet. Sometimes it seems like a good idea, and at other times, I want something else."

"Like what?"

Johnny chuckled. "That's the problem. I don't know what. But I need to decide quickly because my term is ending soon, and my superiors are pressuring me to re-up."

"Then just make a decision. It's not difficult. Yes or no."

"Just like that, huh? It's not so easy," Johnny said.

Michele ordered hot tea, then returned to the conversation. "Let me help you make up your mind."

"And how are you going to do that?"

"You go out with me three more times in the next two weeks, and you'll either want to stay in California with me or you won't."

"Really?" Johnny's smile stretched a mile. "And if I do want to stay? Then what?"

"Then we have to see if I want you to stay," Michele said. "If I do, the matter's solved. If I don't, you can re-up."

Johnny shook his head slowly. "I don't know. I . . ."

"What have you got to lose?" Michele asked. "All you're risking is three dates with me, and they aren't that bad, are they?"

"No, not at all," Johnny said. He reached out his hand to seal the deal. "You've got yourself a bargain. I can see now you must be a good marketing manager."

The waiter came by the table—for the third time—and asked if he could take their order.

"I think we better order this time," Johnny said. "Either that or be thrown out."

Michele didn't need any time. "I'll have the Linguini & Shrimp with extra cheese sprinkled on it, please. And let me have the house salad."

"And I'll have the Filet Mignon, medium and a side of mushrooms, please."

"And the salad, sir?"

"Oh, the house salad is fine."

Two hours later, they left the restaurant and kissed goodnight in the parking lot. "I'll call you tomorrow," Johnny said.

"Only this time, dinner is on me. I know a place in Dana Point that is really good. It's called Luciano's, and I've never had a bad meal there."

"Sounds good, but I've got to warn you, my aunt cooked the best Italian food I've eaten, so I may be hard to please."

"Bring an appetite, and you won't be disappointed."

As they got into their respective cars, Michele blew him a kiss. "See you tomorrow, Johnny."

He waved. "Yeah, see ya," he said.

THREE FOR THREE

The first two dates with Michele went great, much better than Johnny anticipated. She was everything he hoped for and more. In fact, the first few times he went out with her, he did his best to find things wrong with her. Areas where she didn't measure up to Liz or his general expectations.

If she had any faults, he'd either overlooked them or forgotten them because, to him, she was near perfect. She was smart, clever, witty, had a great sense of humor, and—very important to Johnny —she was always in a good mood. She had a positive outlook on life that was contagious. The fact that she was gorgeous only added to her charm.

The morning of the third date, Johnny was a bundle of nerves. He had truly had a great time with Michele, and he really liked her, but his decision was almost made. He'd put too much into the Marines to quit now. He hadn't even used his marksmanship skills, and that was something that was important to him.

At one point, he thought. *Maybe they'll station me here at Pendleton.* But the next thought brought reality. *Doing what? Shooting middle-aged hippies from LA?*

He knew the realism. If he was going to get a chance to use his skills, it would be overseas in an area experiencing conflict. He wasn't happy with his decision. Hell, he didn't even know if it *was* his decision, but he was leaning in that direction.

He dressed in his finest street clothes, then headed out to meet Michele. He had plenty of time to get there, but he didn't want to rush. He needed time to think.

He pulled into Luciano's a few minutes early, parked, and went inside. The maître d' was so good, he recognized Johnny from the previous visit and greeted him by name, though he used his Italian name of Gianni, not Johnny. He showed him to a secluded table and had a waiter bring wine.

Michele showed up within minutes, wearing her usual smile. "Good evening, fine sir," she said.

"You have a good day?" Johnny asked.

"Always," she said, "but I do have an awkward item to bring up."

Johnny seemed surprised. "Bring it up, then. I'm ready."

"I've been offered a promotion to another part of the country. It's a nice promotion, but I don't want to take it if it means breaking off our relationship."

"I'm flattered you'd say that, Michele. But since you did, I'll give you my advice. I think we should stay here."

"*We?* As in you and me together?"

"*We* as in Mr. and Mrs. McCoy." Johnny said.

Michele shook her head. "Whoa. Slow down, Johnny. I was hoping you'd want to stay, but I wasn't expecting this."

"I know a lady who told me decisions weren't hard to make; they were yes or no. Something like that."

Michele laughed. "I think I know that lady," she said.

"I can name a million reasons why this is a bad idea—"

"Like what?"

"Like . . . I've only known you for a couple weeks. I've known the temp at my office longer than you. I know nothing about your family." Michele drank some water, then placed her hands on the table and leaned on her elbows. "By the way, how the heck old are you? Maybe I should ask how *young* are you?"

Johnny hesitated, then said, "Twenty-one."

Michele shook her head. "Oh, my God! I'm robbing the cradle."

"How's that?" Johnny asked. "You can't be much older."

She stared. "Johnny, I'm twenty-seven."

"Does it matter?" Johnny asked. "For me, it doesn't. I don't care how old you are. What matters is how we get along, and I think we get along great."

Michele said, "I'll give it thought." She sipped her wine, then said, "Okay, I've given it thought. Let's do it."

Johnny leaned over and kissed her. "I love you, Michele."

Michele stopped and stared. "That's the first time anyone has told me that since my parents died."

"Get used to it," Johnny said. "It won't be the last."

A NEW COMMITMENT

WINTER, 2005, SOUTHERN CALIFORNIA

Johnny told the colonel of his decision to leave the Marines the following day. "I can stay until my term is up, Colonel, but once that time comes, I'm gone."

"Got somewhere to go?" Colonel Rogers asked.

"Getting married, sir. Met a local and we . . . well, you know."

The colonel laughed. "Yes, Sergeant, I know. It happened to me as well."

Johnny finished out the week and met Michele on Friday night. They ate a light meal at her place, then sat in the living room and chatted.

"I put in for my vacation today," she said. "They were happy for us even though they said I would be sorely missed during that honeymoon time. I told them they'd manage fine without me for a few weeks, but I *had* to go. Call of the wild and all."

Johnny laughed. "I told the colonel earlier this week. He was fine with it too."

"Do we get married here or in Cleveland? I don't care either way, so you decide."

Johnny seemed to give it thought, then said, "I think here. I'd rather go back home already wed. Besides, the only ones I'd really want there are Uncle Dom and Aunt Clorinda, and of course, Tony and Ronnie."

Johnny then shifted on the sofa and turned to face Michele. "There is one thing I never told you about Liz though. And I need you to know before we go any further."

Michele got a rotten feeling in her gut, like she was going to be told someone died. She prepared herself for the worst. "So what is it? She was gorgeous, stunning, unsurpassable, impossible to compete with? What?"

Johnny looked straight at her. "When I told you the killer shot her for no reason, that wasn't quite the truth. He shot her because she was black," he said.

Michele laughed. "That's it? She was black? Who the hell cares? What does it matter?"

Relief washed over Johnny. He smiled, then leaned over and kissed Michele. "And that's why I love you," he said.

Michele smiled back. "If that's the only reason, we've got a problem."

"Well, it's not the only reason," Johnny said. "You do have that nice ass."

The next two weeks went by slowly for Johnny. It seemed as if his term would never end.

Michele said she felt the same way and couldn't wait to get wed. "I'm tired of living a life of sin."

On Friday night, though, his term did end as did her two-week notice of vacation. They celebrated by going out for dinner and retiring at her place. "You better get used to sleeping here," Michele said. "Since you don't have a place anymore, that is."

"Sleeping here does have a few benefits," Johnny said. "Which brings up a point. When are we getting married?"

"Next week," Michele said. "At least, it better be, since I took vacation starting today. After that, I guess it's off to Cleveland so you can show me off."

"I doubt it," Johnny said. "I invited Uncle Dom and his family, but Aunt Clorinda said he was having a few health issues. Nothing to worry about she said, but enough that he probably won't make the wedding. Since they were the only ones that mattered as far as the wedding goes, we can just wait until we go back there on our own."

"And I had my mind made up to discover a new part of the country. What's Cleveland like?"

Johnny nodded. "It's not anything like California, but I think you'll like it. We do have good restaurants there."

Michele shrugged. "What more could a woman ask for—a young and vigorous husband and good restaurants. Life is good."

Johnny playfully slapped her butt. "You're such an ass."

"You seem to like it," she said, then ran from the room.

THE HONEYMOON

By mid-week, Johnny and Michele were Mr. and Mrs. McCoy, and they celebrated by going to dinner and then going to her place and packing. "We don't need to pack much," Michele said. "We're only going to San Francisco; besides, the less we pack, the more I can buy there."

"You're such an—"

"Ass. I know. You love talking about my ass, don't you?"

Johnny came up behind her and squeezed her butt cheeks. "I like doing more than talking about it, young lady."

Michele playfully spun away. "Save those dirty thoughts for after we check in to the hotel. I want to make love while staring over the bay."

"In that case, I'll accommodate you," Johnny said. "Let's get moving."

Johnny had never driven the Pacific Coast Highway from LA to San Francisco, so Michele suggested they drive instead of fly. "It's not a bad drive," she said, "and it's more than gorgeous. If you've never taken the drive, you *have* to."

"How long does it take?"

"Depending on how curious you are about things on the way, anywhere from ten to fourteen hours."

"What? We've got hotel reservations."

"We can change them by one night. I promise, it's worth it."

Johnny smiled. "All right. I guess I'll have to trust you."

The drive turned out to be everything Michele said it would be— maybe even more. "I can tell you one thing. We're definitely coming back here. There were too many places I missed."

"You'll want to make at least two more stops," Michele said. "The first is to see the Hearst Castle, and the second is Monterrey. After that, it's not far to the city."

They stopped for almost two hours at the castle, then spent another two hours in Monterrey and checked into the Grand Hyatt around seven that evening.

For two weeks, Johnny and Michele roamed the city with reckless abandonment, soaking in plays, the theater, and concerts galore, and exploring a host of restaurants in North Beach and China-town. When the time came to leave, neither one of them wanted to go. "I could stay here forever," Johnny said.

"If you do, you'll have to fly to LA to see me because that's where I'll be."

Johnny kissed her. "And you know I'd never do that, spoiled lady."

A knock on the door sounded, then the bellhop announced he was there to get their bags. "Say goodbye to San Francisco," Michele said.

The drive back was much shorter because they didn't take the coastal drive, although Johnny promised they would do that again and soon. Back in LA, they settled in for the weekend, both eager to start a new life and dreading having to return to work.

For the first few weeks of married life, Michele and Johnny barely saw each other. She was swamped with work after being away for three weeks, and he was occupied trying to find a new job.

On week three after being home, Johnny landed a position as a salesman for a computer company. It wasn't something he was experienced in, but the sales manager said they would train him.

"You'll fit right in," he said. "Selling isn't much more than learning how to listen. I think you'll do fine."

For the first few months, Johnny's sales were far above average, and after that, they moved even higher. It wasn't difficult to sell the computers. People needed and wanted computers, so they sold themselves. All Johnny had to do was listen and counter any objections. To top it off, commissions were great. He soon was earning almost as much as Michele, and between the two of them, they had a lot of extra income.

On Friday night, Michele surprised Johnny by greeting him at the door with an invitation to dinner at a fancy local restaurant. "What's the occasion?" Johnny asked. "Did you get promoted?"

"No," Michele said. "You're just that special."

"Well, I guess I can't argue with that," he said, and they both laughed.

At the restaurant, after wine was served, Michele said, "Johnny, we make enough money now, I think it's time we thought about starting a family. I'm not getting any younger, you know."

Johnny beamed. "Fantastic. I'd love it. When are you thinking about doing it?"

"I don't know," Michele said. "Maybe a month ago."

Johnny appeared confused, then his face lit up with recognition. "You're pregnant! Now?"

She nodded her head and smiled, then held a finger to her lips. "Johnny, be quiet. We don't want to announce this to the world."

"The hell we don't," Johnny said, then he stood and held the wine glass in the air. "Attention, everyone. My lovely wife and I are expecting our first baby."

People at tables all around cheered and saluted or tapped silverware on their glasses. "Congratulations," rang out from almost every table.

Johnny sat back down, leaned over, and kissed Michele. "I'm so damn happy I could cry."

Michele used a handkerchief to dry her eyes. "I *am* crying," she said.

IT'S A GIRL

SPRING 2006, SOUTHERN CALIFORNIA

Johnny returned from a long day of travel, parked his car, and went inside. He walked through the front door, only to be greeted by blaring horns and pink balloons.

"A girl?" he shouted. "You got the results?"

Michele jumped up and hugged him. "A girl. And the doc said everything looks great."

"I couldn't be happier," Johnny said. "Another you."

Michele kissed him warmly. "I'm the second luckiest woman in the world," she said.

"The second?"

Michele patted her stomach. "Yes, the first is this little bundle of joy I'm carrying because she gets to have you for a daddy."

∽

Michele worked for five more months, then she announced she'd be taking maternity leave. Fortunately, her firm supported such things, and they were more than generous—allowing six months of time off, with the provision Michele called in to offer consulting advice when needed.

The baby was born just after Thanksgiving, and everything went well. She was seven pounds, twenty inches, and she seemed healthy as hell. Johnny was ecstatic.

They decided to name her Clorinda after Johnny's aunt, although they called her Chloe. When they called to tell Aunt Clorinda, she couldn't stop crying.

For the first three months, Michele found it difficult to compete with Johnny for time with the baby. He doted on her from the time he came home at night until he left in the morning.

Michele thought she may have a hard time getting him to change diapers or get up for nightly feedings, but he did it with no qualms or complaints. And best of all, he was good at it. If Chloe was fussy, she calmed down almost instantly when Johnny picked her up.

On weekends, Johnny took Michele and Chloe to the beach or the zoo, or any number of places, but no matter what, they always had a good time. Life couldn't get any better.

Six months after Chloe was born, they found an outstanding sitter to watch her, and Michele went back to work. She had extended her maternity leave by months, but her bosses didn't mind. They wanted her that badly.

Johnny also was doing great, registering as the number three salesman in the country two years in a row.

Johnny got up early on Saturday morning and was cooking break-fast when Chloe walked in, wiping sleep from her eyes. "Where are we going today, Daddy? How about the zoo?"

"If you can tell me what's cooking without peeking, I might consider it."

Chloe laughed. "That's easy, Daddy. It's sausage and eggs."

"Then I guess we're going to the zoo," Johnny said. "Go wake up Mrs. sleepy head."

Johnny and his family spent all day Saturday at the San Diego zoo, then all day Sunday at the Santa Monica beach. Around six o'clock on Sunday evening, Chloe crashed, falling asleep before they got home. After tucking her into bed, Michele came back to the living room. "I would have given a million dollars to have had a childhood like hers. She's one lucky girl."

Johnny nodded. "And I would have given ten million."

For two more years, life was great. Michele thrived at her job, and Johnny continued to do well as a salesman. Best of all, Chloe improved in every area possible.

One morning, Michele scanned the papers for something special to get Johnny for a fifth anniversary, when she saw something that caught her eye, but not in a good way.

She read the morning paper with her breakfast every morning, but today, an article on page three caught her eye and caused her to stop. She read the article twice, then folded the page and put it in her purse. It was something she'd have to discuss with Johnny at dinner.

Michele came home from work and surprised Johnny by taking him out to dinner at his favorite restaurant. She had arranged a sitter for Chloe, so there were no concerns there.

They were seated at a table she had reserved near the back, then the waiter brought wine.

"What a night," Johnny said. "As usual, you outdid yourself."

"Thank you, dear, but I have something you need to see. I hesitate to bring it up before dinner, but I think you should see it."

What she said made Johnny curious as hell. "What is it?"

She reached into her purse and removed the folded piece of newspaper. "Read the article below the fold," she said.

He quickly looked, and it caught his eye immediately.

SERIAL KILLER STRIKES AGAIN IN CLEVELAND

The killer, once thought gone, seems to have returned. There is always a chance it's a copycat killer, but sources high up in the department indicate otherwise. For the second time this week, a young black woman has been shot and killed from long distance. The distance alone rules out the majority of suspects. It would require a marksman of some skill. The killings began several years ago and claimed the lives of four young black women. A few months later, they mysteriously stopped and then started up again. Now they have begun a third time.

Johnny read it three times before setting the paper on the table. "Son of a bitch," he said. "The bastard is at it again."

"When I read that, I knew you'd want to see it," Michele said.

"You were right," Johnny said, "And this makes up my mind."

"About what?" Michele asked.

"I need to find this son of a bitch and stop him. Stop him permanently."

"And you're going to do that all by yourself?"

"I didn't say that, but I *am* going to do it. I guarantee it. I think we should go to Cleveland. I'll become a cop and get this thing solved once and for all."

WELCOME HOME, JOHNNY

2010, SOUTHERN CALIFORNIA

Johnny and Michele decided to sell her furniture, only keeping things she felt sentimental about. When they were ready, they started out for Cleveland, taking a scenic route that allowed them to see things they both had on a wish list—the Grand Canyon, Pikes Peak, Bryce Canyon, and so much more.

It was a roundabout way to get to Cleveland, but they got there eventually, pulling into a hotel six days after leaving LA. They could have made the drive in two days, but the extra time was worth it. They now had memories to last years.

It was already getting dark when they pulled into the city. Michele spoke in almost a whisper because Chloe was sleeping. "Where should we spend the night? We can't pester your folks at this time."

"How about one final splurge? The Hyatt isn't far from here, and it's great. It's not far from the lake, it has a fantastic restaurant, and it's just a gorgeous hotel."

"You've sold me," Michele said. "Let's do it."

They checked in, tucked Chloe in bed, and ordered a late dinner via room service. "Ordinarily, I'm not fond of room service for meals," Michele said, "but this was delicious." She then stepped into the hall and looked out over the lobby. "And you weren't kidding about it being gorgeous. This is stunning," she said.

After a marvelous sleep and an even more marvelous lovemaking session, Johnny and Michele had breakfast and showed Chloe around the hotel. Afterward, as they walked to the room, Michele said, "I know we have to leave, but I don't want to. I could spend a few months--or even a few years--at this place."

Johnny nodded. "I agree, but my savings aren't quite that extensive, so we'll have to check out." He picked up Chloe and hugged her. "Besides," he said, "I know my sweetie wants her own house with a playground and maybe even a dog." He nuzzled noses with her and said, "Don't you, sweetie?"

"And I want a *big* dog, Daddy. Like the one we saw at the zoo."

Michele laughed. "Chloe, that was a wolf, honey, not a dog. But they do have dogs that look similar. Daddy will have to check it out."

Michele took Chloe from Johnny's arms as he opened the door to their room. "I guess we better get going, Johnny. We need to go see Aunt Clorinda and Uncle Dom."

"Aunt Clorinda? Clorinda is *my* name," Chloe said.

Michele hugged her close and smiled. "Yes, it is. And you were named after Aunt Clorinda. She is Daddy's aunt, but she raised him like a mother."

"Oh, boy," Chloe said. "I can't wait to meet her."

"And you're gonna love them," Johnny said. "They're nice people."

"They must be nice if they had the patience to raise you," Michele said.

Johnny parked on the street, and he and Michele walked to the front door and knocked. Aunt Clorinda answered within seconds, stepping back and gasping when she saw them. "Johnny! My God, what are you doing here?" She turned and hollered. "Dom, Dom, get in here."

Uncle Dom walked into the living room, then rushed to welcome them into the house.

"And who is this beautiful young woman?" Clorinda said as she stooped to pinch Chloe's cheeks.

Johnny stepped aside and said, "This beautiful young woman is Clorinda, also known as Chloe, McCoy."

"What? How's that possible?" Clorinda asked. "That's my name. Did you steal my name, little girl?"

Chloe glanced at her mother and father, looking confused.

Uncle Dom stepped in and picked her up. "Pay no attention to your Aunt Clorinda. She was just teasing you. Now come on, let's go to the kitchen and see if we can find any special treats for you. What do you like?"

Johnny shook his head. "What happened to the strict disciplinarian who raised me? When was he replaced by that softy?"

Aunt Clorinda shrugged. "He's always been a sucker for little kids, Johnny." She then turned to Michele, hugged her, and kissed her cheeks. "Welcome to the family, dear. Now, lets go to the kitchen. I'll see what we can make for supper while Dom is spoiling Chloe."

Johnny shook his head. "Didn't I tell you, Michele? She's always worried about food."

They talked for hours and by mid-afternoon Clorinda was getting nervous. "Where the hell are those boys? I called them ages ago."

"Tony and Ronnie don't live here now?" Johnny asked.

"They moved out about six months ago," Dom said. "Ronnie has an apartment on the west side, and Tony is living with his girlfriend not far from him."

About five o'clock, Tony and Ronnie showed up, and they had the necessary items from Rubino's. I think that's all that mattered to Aunt Clorinda. She immediately got to cooking, and while she cooked, Ronnie and Tony played with Chloe. "Do you know your daddy used to live here?" Tony asked.

"Really?" she said. "In this house?"

"Yep," Ronnie said. "We grew up together."

"Do you need any help?" Michele asked Clorinda.

Clorinda waved her hand in the air, as if to brush her off. "I'll have none of that nonsense. Just sit and talk. And don't forget to correct all of their lies those men tell—*if* you can catch them all."

Michele laughed and whispered to Johnny. "She's a character."

"That she is," Johnny said.

Dom and Clorinda filled Johnny in on the family and what had transpired since he was gone. "Brandon's been by a few times to see if we'd heard from you, but I told him we hadn't. You should give him a call though. He seemed worried."

"Speaking of Brandon reminds me, Uncle Dom. What news is there on the serial killer? Anything new? Michele noticed an article in the LA paper that he started up again."

Dom shook his head. "It's true, Johnny. And they don't have a clue about who it is or why he's doing it."

Clorinda seemed disgusted. "We know darn right well *why* he's doing it. He's doing it because they're black. You don't need to be a detective to know that."

"I don't know," Dom mumbled.

"Well, *I* know," Clorinda said.

"Uncle Dom, I want to join the force," Johnny said. "Can you help me with that?"

"Be a cop? What in God's name do you want to do that for?" Aunt Clorinda asked. "You can do so many things that are better. I used to think being a cop was good, but after being married to one for so long, I have doubts."

Aunt Clorinda turned to Michele. "What about you, dear? What do you do?"

She laughed. "Right now nothing. But I used to be a marketing manager for an advertising company."

"Now *that's* a good occupation, Johnny." Aunt Clorinda wagged her finger, as if scolding him. "Take a lesson from your wife and find something like that." Clorinda looked back at Michele and said, "There should be plenty of jobs in advertising, Michele. Dom has a cousin who is a director at Selkor and Taylor. I'm sure he could introduce you."

Johnny didn't roll his eyes, but he felt as if he should. "Aunt Clorinda, we—"

"That would be great, Clorinda. I'd love to meet him," Michele said. "Selkor and Taylor is an excellent firm, and it would be fortunate just to get in to see someone."

"Good," Aunt Clorinda said, then looked at her husband. "Dom, give Art a call tomorrow and see if he can set something up."

Johnny cleared his throat in an obvious attempt to draw attention. "As I was asking, Uncle Dom, can you help with me joining the force?"

"I don't know if I can do much good, but you should talk to Bob."

"Uncle Bob? As in Aunt Trudy's husband?"

"One and the same," Dom said. "Bob now works in personnel, so he might have some stroke. I'll talk to him, but you should too. He'd be glad to hear from you."

"Great," Johnny said. "I'll give him a call tomorrow.

When Johnny and Michele left the house, Dom followed them outside. He pulled Johnny aside and whispered, "When you talk to Bob, you might ask him about the serial killer. I don't know if he knows any more than I do, but I'd bet he has access to files that can tell him."

"Okay, great, Uncle Dom. Thanks."

ANOTHER NEW LIFE

Johnny called Bob first thing in the morning, but Trudy said he had already left for work. "Let me give you his direct line at work, Johnny. You got a pen to write this down?"

"I'm ready, Aunt Trudy."

"Okay, it's 555-9322. And it's so good to hear from you again. You need to stop by. Bob would be thrilled. Besides, you've got to show off that gorgeous little girl. All we've seen are pictures."

"Okay, we will."

"Tell me when so I can cook something up."

Johnny covered up the mouthpiece, looked over to Michele, and whispered, "Tomorrow night?"

She nodded, so he got back on the phone with Trudy. "How about tomorrow night?"

"Perfect. See you at seven. Or is that too late for Chloe?"

"Seven is fine, Aunt Trudy. See you then. And I can't wait to taste your cooking again."

Johnny hung up the phone, already shaking his head.

"Everyone sounds excited to see you, Johnny. Is her cooking as good as Clorinda's?"

"That's why I shook my head. We'll need to eat *before* arriving, and then nibble on her food and pretend it's good because it doesn't come close to Aunt Clorinda's. In fact, if there is an opposite to her cooking, Trudy has nailed it."

Michele made a face. "Johnny, it can't be that bad."

Johnny laughed. "It *can* be, and it is. Wait and see. I just hope Chloe doesn't give it away."

They showed up at Trudy's a few minutes before seven, and after all the greetings and introductions, they sat down to eat.

"Looks good," Michele said, taking a seat next to Bob.

Bob smiled as he looked at Johnny. "I can't believe how damn big you are now. And how much you've filled out." He then turned to Michele and nudged her. "When this little shit joined up, he was skinny as a rail and a good three inches shorter. I kid you not." Bob then reached over and pinched Chloe's cheeks. "And this little sweetie pie. Look how beautiful she is. And how *big*."

Trudy nodded while chewing. "It's true, Michele. And when Bob says Johnny was skinny, he means it. I'd say he's put on fifty pounds, and it looks as if it's all muscle."

Johnny blushed. "You're close, Aunt Trudy. I added forty-five pounds."

Bob got serious all of a sudden. "I saw you called work earlier, Johnny, but I was in meetings all day. I did speak to Dom though, and he told me you're interested in joining the force."

"I am, Uncle Bob. Can you help with that?"

"I can't swear to it, but probably. But know that I mean 'probably' as in I might be able to get you an interview. After that, it's up to you. I can't and won't do anything to get you on the force; in other words, if you get in, it's going to be on your own. Understand?"

Johnny nodded. "I wouldn't expect anything else, Uncle Bob. And thanks. Just getting an interview is more than I hoped for."

"When are you thinking about joining?"

"Right away," Johnny said. "As soon as we can make it happen."

"I'll get on it right away," Bob said. "Anything else?"

Johnny hesitated, then said, "There is one more thing, Uncle Bob. Is there any way you can help me look into the serial killer?"

"When you say 'look into,' what are you referring to?"

"I mean getting me access to any files or information that I otherwise wouldn't have."

"Damn, Johnny, I don't know. It would be against policy."

"I'm not asking you to *give* me the files, Uncle Bob. I just need copies, or even a half hour to look at them. No one would ever know."

Trudy interrupted. "Johnny, you know Bob can't do that. I'm surprised that you asked."

"Just look at them? That's all you'd need?" Bob asked.

"That will work," Johnny said. "It would mean a lot."

"Let me think about it," Bob said. "I'll see what I can do."

Trudy served dessert—cannoli she picked up from Rubino's—and while we were eating, Bob spoke up. "I've got an idea. Suppose when you come for your interview, I arrange it so that I'm the one to show you around, and while we're doing that, I could let you view the files. They'd have to go right back though. They can't leave the area."

Johnny got excited. "Uncle Bob, that would be perfect. I can't thank you enough."

"You can thank me by never telling anybody about this. If the brass found out, I'd be canned in a New York minute."

"Don't worry," Johnny said, "the Marines trained me in how to resist torture from our overseas enemies. I can't imagine the CPD could be worse."

"All right," Bob said. "Be ready in two to three days. It won't take longer than that to arrange an interview."

"What? That quick? What do I need to know? Any suggestions?"

"I don't think you have a problem with physical abilities and definitely not with marksmanship. The mental capacity should be a breeze. I think the only part they'll press you on is how your mother died. They'll know all about it since your father was on the force, so I'd be prepared to answer questions about that."

"How should I handle those?"

"Don't brush them over. Don't ignore them. Just show the sorrow you feel but add that you've learned to deal with it. That it bothered you for a long while, but living with a loving family like Dom and Clorinda and then going into the Marines helped a lot."

"And you think that will do it?" Johnny asked.

"They can't ask for much more," Bob said. "Don't worry. You'll do fine."

Johnny and Michele finished out the evening, but when Chloe began yawning, a sure sign she was about to fall asleep, Johnny announced it was time to go home. 'Home' was a one-bedroom apartment on the west side of the city; in fact, it wasn't too far from where Tony and Ronnie lived.

Johnny tucked Chloe in, then he and Michele settled in for the night. She leaned over and kissed him, then asked, "Are you sure this is what you want to do?"

"I'm sure. Why do you ask?"

"I just wonder, why you would want to be a cop after all you've been through with your father—him being a cop and doing what he did?"

Johnny nodded. "I know what you mean, but what he did had nothing to do with being a cop. Not a good cop anyway. He was the kind of person who gave cops a bad name. Some still do, but most of them are good, like Uncle Dom. He's a great cop, and everybody I know likes him."

A NEW JOB

Two days later, Johnny got a call from the CPD, asking if he could come for an interview the next day. He arranged to be there at nine. After visiting several officers and numerous patrolmen, he was shown to the captain's office. The captain grilled him for almost an hour, focusing mostly on his experience in the Marines and on why he wanted to be on the force.

"I would think after what happened with your father that being on the force would be the last thing you'd want."

Johnny thought for a moment before answering. "You might think so at first, Captain. But it worked the other way around with me. I've got three uncles who are also on the force, and they are all good cops. Good people too. I want to be like them and make sure that Cleveland cops keep a good reputation. My mother used to say, you can't let one bad apple spoil the bunch, and I guess I believe that."

"I like that," the captain said. "It's what I was looking for. Now let me deliver you to one of those good uncles of yours. He'll finish out the day with you."

I met Uncle Bob, and he showed me around the different departments. He must have introduced me to a dozen more people while we were at it too. Finally—after navigating what seemed like a maze—we made it up to where the files were kept. Bob checked that no one was around, then he got me what I needed.

"Clock's ticking, Johnny. You don't have long."

Johnny began reading the files, going as fast as he could.

After a moment, Bob grabbed the folder and set it on the table. "Here, let me have that," Bob said.

"I'm not finished yet," Johnny said.

"And at that rate you never will be." He pulled a phone from his pocket and snapped pictures, flipping pages as he did. "I'm gonna give you these pictures, but if you ever tell—"

Johnny smiled. "Don't worry, Uncle Bob. I won't."

Johnny thanked Bob and then went home to look at what he'd gotten. He got back to the apartment, all charged up from the excitement of the day. He felt good about the interviews he had, and he even felt good about his meeting with the captain. Best of all though, was how Uncle Bob helped him out by giving him pictures of the files.

Johnny had two days of grueling testing. First was the written exam which he already knew he scored high on, then the physical agility test. Compared to what he endured in the Marines, it was easy. Next came the polygraph and psychology exams. He wasn't worried about the polygraph, but he had concerns regarding the psychology. He knew it would include questions about his father. How they interpreted his answers was anybody's guess. After that, all that remained was the medical, which he felt sure he would ace.

After completing the tests, he went home with a smile on his face.

"How did it go?" Michele asked.

"I think it went great. I guess we'll see when we hear back from them." Johnny sat down beside her and put his arm on her shoulder. "And you, my marketing genius? How did it go with you?"

"If you mean the introduction from Dom? It went much better than expected; in fact, Art knows the company I worked for and asked if he could call for a reference."

"Looks like we both had good days," Johnny said, then he glanced around, almost as if in a panic. "And what about my sweetie? Where is she?"

"That's more good news," Michele said. "I found a sitter right here in the complex, and not only is she great, there are lots of other kids her age to play with; in fact, she's out on the playground now." Michele walked to the window and pulled the drapes aside. "Look, Johnny. Look how much fun she's having."

Johnny smiled. "God, I love that little devil. She's so damn adorable."

"That she is," Michele said as she lay her head on Johnny's shoulder. "That she is."

After dinner, Johnny spent hours going through the files. Some things he understood and others he didn't. One thing was clear though; CPD had no idea what was going on. One reference mentioned a copycat killer, and another said it was the same guy. Without specifics, Johnny wasn't going to be able to make heads or tails from this. He needed help.

The next day, he pored over the files again, but to no avail, so that night he called Uncle Dom after dinner.

"Hey, Johnny. How did it go with Bob? Was he able to do you any good?"

"More than good, Uncle Dom. I've already had my interview with the department, and Bob helped in other ways as well."

"Good. I'm glad. So what can I do for you?"

"Bob gave me some things to look at, but I can't decipher it all. I thought maybe you could help."

"Now we're getting into territory I *can* help with. How about tomorrow night? You, Michele, and Chloe can come for dinner or you can come afterward. Whichever you prefer."

"You know I love Aunt Clorinda's cooking, Uncle Dom, but let's plan on after dinner. I promised Michele I'd take her out to celebrate and Chloe is going to her first sleepover ever, and Michele wants to stay close in case she gets nervous."

"I know what you mean there," Dom said. "I still remember Tony's first ventures at spending the night. It took us three times before he was able to stay at anyone's house. And you said 'celebrate.' What are you celebrating? Am I going to be a great uncle again?"

Johnny laughed. "No, Uncle Dom. We're not expecting. I'd have told you guys if we were. We're celebrating because we *think*— emphasis on think—that it looks positive for both of us to get a job."

"Sounds great, Johnny, but if not, we've always got room. You know that."

"Thanks, Uncle Dom. You guys are the best."

"Yeah, yeah. I'll see you tomorrow night."

Johnny showed up at Dom's house around eight, and Dom led him to the kitchen table where they spread out the files and got to work.

Dom took a moment to familiarize himself with the first few. "Man, they've got a lot of data on this guy already. I'm surprised there hasn't been more headway."

"When you say a lot of data, what does that mean? What do they know?"

"For instance," Dom said. "They've determined the shots were taken from at least a couple hundred yards, which means we've got a real marksman, not some weekend shooter."

"A couple of hundred yards eliminates a lot of people, but it leaves a lot as suspects too."

"I understand that," Dom said, "but it also makes you wonder why. *Why* is the guy doing this? He's not getting sexual gratification from it. So *why* is he doing it?"

"Come on, Uncle Dom, that part is obvious—because they're black. All the girls he killed were black. And don't tell me it could be coincidence because it couldn't. Not with that many people being killed."

Dom nodded. "I know what you think, Johnny, but we can't make assumptions. We've got no proof."

"I understand what you're saying, Uncle Dom, but if there's one thing I learned in the Marines, it's to gather the data, interpret the data, then make a decision."

Uncle Dom nodded. "All I know so far is that the shooter was a long way out, like I said, a couple hundred yards."

"I know what you said, Uncle Dom, but we need to know a lot more than that. I need to know if the same gun fired all the shots, what kind of gun fired the shots, and ideally, where the ammo came from."

"That's a lot to know, Johnny."

"I realize that, Uncle Dom, but a lot is at stake."

"I'll see what I can find out, but I've got to be careful too. They're keeping a tight lid on this, and I'm too close to retirement to mess up." Uncle Dom stood, signaling it was time to go. "If I were you, Johnny, I'd start by looking into anyone who could make a shot from that far out. I'll try to get you more information in the meantime."

"All right. Thanks, Uncle Dom. I'll get busy."

"Do it, but don't be caught looking into it. You're a fresh recruit. They'll can your ass without thinking about it."

WHERE TO START?

Johnny sat with Michele and drank his coffee early in the morning. He had just gotten Chloe off to school, and he sat back down and stared out the window. He loved watching the trees in the park as they blew in the wind.

"What's on your mind?" Michele asked. "Whenever you stare at the leaves blowing, you're thinking about something. Or worrying."

Johnny snapped out of it and turned to Michele. "I was just thinking that there can't be too many people capable of making a shot like the ones the serial killer made. And I'm even more sure that whoever it is most likely haunts one of the many shooting ranges around the city.

"And how is that going to help?" she asked.

"I'm going to visit the ranges and see who the best shots are."

"All the ranges?" Michele asked. "That amounts to a lot of locations, doesn't it? From what you've told me, it does."

"Not really. Yes, there are a lot of shooting ranges, but not all of them specialize in long-range weapons. I need to focus on the ones that do—at least, I'll start with them."

"You can't just walk up and ask for the names of the best shots."

Johnny thought a moment. "No, but I could stage a competition. Maybe I can convince CPD to allow me and a few others to challenge any shooter."

"Why would the shooter expose himself?" Michele asked.

"I think he'd do it for the challenge alone, but I might be able to get the captain to put up a prize as well. I think for the combination, he'd definitely do it."

"If you think it will work, I'd give it a shot," Michele said. "I like the idea. It's imaginative."

"I doubt if the captain will think so, but we'll see. I'll sell it to him somehow."

Michele made a bagel to go along with her tea. As she sat back down, she said, "Maybe you could sell him on doing it as a stunt for good publicity. The department is always looking for good publicity, isn't it? In this day and age, almost all police departments are. This would be a chance to get some."

Johnny nodded slowly. "I like it, Michele. Something like that just might work."

She smiled at Johnny. "Then put on your sales hat and get in there and sell him on it. You've already shown what a good salesman you are in California. All you need to do is switch gears; instead of selling a product, you're selling an idea. Remember, selling is all about convincing a person they need something. Whether it's a computer, a phone, or an ice cream cone, it's all the same."

Johnny pulled her close and kissed her. "You're pretty smart, you know that?"

"Yes, *I* know that, and it's about time you realized it."

Johnny got in a few minutes early and put in a request to see Captain Helger. Ten minutes later, he was shown in to his office. "You wanted to see me, McCoy?"

"Sir, I did. I had an idea that I thought you might be interested in it."

"Go on."

"I've been reading in the paper all the negativity about the force, sir. And I thought we might do something to change that—get people fired up and excited about the CPD."

"What did you have in mind? The people of Cleveland aren't idiots. They're not going to fall for a parade or a carnival or some such nonsense."

"No, sir. I understand that. I was thinking of us holding a shooting contest. The CPD will have two shooters who will take on all comers. Contests will be with targets at fifty, one hundred, two hundred, and five hundred yards."

"Suppose it's a tie?" Helger asked.

"In the event of a tie, whoever wins the five-hundred yard contest wins the event."

"I don't know," he said. "What if we lose? And there's a good chance of that with so many nuts who frequent shooting ranges around here."

"Sir, there's always that possibility, but if the department has even one good marksman, I don't think we'll lose."

"Why only one? I thought you said the department would be represented by two shooters?"

"Sir, not to brag, but I went through sniper school in the Marines and served for four years afterward. I feel confident I can beat almost anyone out there."

"How good were you?" the captain asked.

"I came in second in sniper school," Johnny said.

The captain laughed. "So you're looking to stack the deck?"

Johnny shrugged, but the captain spoke again. "No, I like the idea, and I like you being in it even more. Let's plan on it. I'll have public relations get the word out and set it in motion. Do you have anyone in mind for the second shooter?"

"No, sir. I don't. I know a few good shots, but I have no idea how they'd stack up. As far as that goes, all three of my uncles are pretty good shots. Dom's probably the worst, but Harry and Bob are very good."

"All right, I'll have someone look into it. As for you, keep those marksman skills sharp. I don't want to lose this damn contest."

"Don't worry, sir. I won't my skills get rusty." Johnny turned to leave, and the captain said.

"You mentioned your uncle's name was Dom? Are you Dom Camino's boy?"

"He's my uncle, yes sir. He was my mother's brother."

"Dom's a good man. Give him my regards. And I'll have Margie get with you on coordinating this contest."

Johnny walked in the apartment, looking dejected. He took off his jacket, tossed it on the couch, and plopped down.

Michele walked over and sat next to him. "What's the matter, Johnny? Bad day?"

Johnny hugged her and smiled. "Actually, it was a great day. Captain Helger bought my idea on the shooting contest—or should I say *your* idea—and is gung ho on me competing in it."

Michele got all excited. "Oh, my God, Johnny. I'm so happy for you. When will it happen?"

"I don't know that yet, but he said he'd have his assistant get in touch with me."

"This is great," Michele said. "What do you have to do to prepare?"

"Nothing much. The captain suggested I keep my skills sharp. I suppose I could do a little practice shooting, which isn't a bad idea anyway. Maybe I can pick up a few leads."

"You have somewhere in mind?"

Johnny nodded. "The range my father used to drag me to as a child. They had a lot of long-range shooters there. Maybe they still do."

Chloe bounded into the living room, being chased by two other girls who looked to be about the same age. They all were laughing and squealing. Johnny looked to Michele. "Does this go on all the time?"

She nodded. "Pretty much. Isn't it great? She's made so many friends in such a short time."

"I love it," Johnny said. "Nothing could make me happier."

LOOKING FOR A SHOOTER

On Saturday morning, Johnny wrote down directions to the range before he left, but he felt sure he wouldn't need them. He still had nightmares of the drive to that place from when his father used to haul him up there on the weekends. Johnny let the memories play in his head as he drove. He saw each intersection and which way to turn, and he felt every bump in the road.

Fifteen minutes later, he pulled into a parking lot that hadn't changed in ten years, other than the make and model of pickup truck that occupied the parking spaces. He looked up as he was about to enter the building and noticed the sign was the same—at least, it looked the same: *Max's Guns and Ammo.*

He walked inside and up to the counter, where a burly old guy with a gray beard waited on people. After he finished with a customer, he turned to Johnny. "What'll it be? Short or long-range? Inside or out?"

Johnny almost smiled—almost. "Long-range for outside. Gun and ammo on the two-hundred yard target."

The man looked at Johnny with a skewed eye. "The two-hundred? You that good, boy?"

"I'll put up ten bucks against anybody you got," Johnny said.

"Make it fifty, and I'll get you someone who'll make you prove those boasts."

Johnny dug into his pocket, pulled out some cash, and counted it. "I can do fifty. Bring your guy on. But give me ten minutes to practice before we compete."

"Any particular gun?"

"Doesn't matter. You pick it, but make sure it's accurate and reliable."

The man smiled like the cat that caught the canary. "My man will be out there in ten minutes. You can't miss him. Big guy with a bald head."

Johnny set the cash on the counter to pay for the rentals, and the guy looked at him. "You sure there's no preference on the gun?"

"Since you're asking again, I guess I might. I don't imagine you ever got any Barrett M82s, did you? If not, I'll take a Remington M24."

The guy stopped and stared at Johnny. "Do I know you? You been here before?"

"It's been a long time, but yeah, my father used to haul my ass out here when I was just a kid. His name was—"

"Mike McCoy," he said. "Sure. I remember now. You were shooting the two-hundred yard targets when you were barely able to carry the rifle. Shit, if I'd have known it was you, I wouldn't have backed the other guy's play. Anyway, good luck. And by the way, sorry about what happened with your mother. That shit ain't right."

"Thanks, Max," Johnny said.

As Johnny walked toward the range, Max hollered, "And take it easy on my boy. Don't embarrass him too much."

About an hour later, Johnny walked back in, toting his rifle and what little ammo he had left. He set them on the counter and waited for Max.

Max walked over wearing a frown. "I don't guess you're reaching for a fifty to pay me," he said.

Johnny smiled and shook his head. "Afraid not, Max. I'd like to say it was close but it wasn't."

Max opened the register and put a fifty on the counter in front of Johnny. "Where have you been all these years? Sure as hell not here. Where have you been taking all your business?"

"The Marines," Johnny said. "I qualified as a sniper, then they sent me all over. Mostly overseas though."

Max slapped his palm to his forehead. "Christ's sake, I should have known. Well, you did good, kid. I'm glad for you. And good to see you again even if it did cost me a few bucks."

Johnny laughed. "Good to see you too, Max. But don't worry, I'll be back."

Johnny hit two more ranges that day, and at each one, he let it be known he was up for a shooting competition. He won another two-hundred-yard competition at the first range, but could only find a taker for one hundred yards at the second range. He won them both handily. He also managed to pick up information on two other ranges where long-range shooting took place regularly, but it was too late in the day to check those out. *They'll have to wait till next week.*

When he entered the apartment that night, Michele was waiting. "And?"

He held out his hand with the cash in it. "One hundred and twenty bucks," he said. "Three for three."

"I expected no less of my sniper husband," Michele said.

Johnny wrapped his arms around her and squeezed. "Is that right?"

She nodded. "I say that because you also hit another target."

He got a confused look on his face, then recognition must have set in. "You're pregnant? You're shitting me?"

Michele laughed and kissed him. "I'm so excited that you're happy."

"What? Of course, I'm happy. We're gonna have another baby. Who the hell wouldn't be happy about a baby?"

THE GAME IS ON

Johnny spent every spare moment the next week practicing his long-range shooting. He went to different ranges, and while he was there, he put out feelers by acting slightly racist.

At a range on the east side of the city, a guy next to him said something after one of Johnny's comments about 'darkies.'

"Hey, bud, ain't you a cop?"

Johnny turned to him and glared. "I am. What of it?"

"That's no way for a damn cop to talk. Hell, that ain't no way for anybody to talk."

"Mister, what I think *off* the job is my own business. All you need to worry about is what I say or do while I'm *on* the job. And if you're really curious, I am *not* on the job now."

Johnny took a half dozen more shots, then packed his things and left. At the next range, he didn't see anyone of interest, so he shot a few dozen rounds and departed. When he got to Max's range, it was crowded. He even had to wait for a slot on the two-hundred-yard range.

He took a position next to a big guy with short, blond hair. After five or six shots, the guy lifted his binoculars and looked at Johnny's target. "Damn good shooting. You come here often?"

Johnny shook his head. "Used to long ago, but I've been gone for years. Just got back."

"When did you shoot here?" the guy asked.

Johnny thought of not answering, but then he said, "Must be fifteen years now. I was away for a while, then I was in the Marines."

"Fifteen years? You don't look that old."

"I'm not. My dad used to bring me. I was only ten at the time."

The guy whistled long and slow. "Goddamn, don't tell me you're Johnny McCoy."

Johnny stopped and looked up. "I am. Who are you?"

The guy held out his hand. "Bobby Reynolds. I used to see you when your dad came to my dad's place to pick up ammo and targets. PJ was his name. Had a place up toward the lake."

Johnny smiled and stood. "Holy crap, I remember. PJ would load his shells, and every week my dad would stop for targets regardless of whether he needed shells."

"Damn straight he did," Bobby said. "And if I remember right, you were a damn good shot back then."

Johnny shook his head again. "I *had* to shoot good or the old man beat me half to death. He didn't tolerate mediocrity."

Bobby nodded. "I know what you mean about that. Mine didn't either."

Johnny looked as if he were thinking, then said, "I don't remember seeing you out there. I'm guessing you'd have been fifteen or sixteen at the time."

"Yeah, we didn't go there. My old man had his own range behind our house. Had dirt mounded up eight or ten feet high and had a fence surrounding that. He said he wasn't about to pay to shoot his gun.

"Son of a gun," Johnny said. "That explains it. I always thought PJ was just on the supply side of the business. Guess he did both."

"He did both all right. He was a good shot in his day. Not much now though. His eyes have gone bad. He can barely reload the ammo."

"You mean he's still in business?"

"Not really. He loads for a few old buddies, and he sells the occasional target, but for the most part, that's just to keep him busy. He's essentially retired."

Johnny nodded. "How about it, Bobby? Want to run down a few for old times' sake."

"I'll shoot twelve shots with you, but I'm not putting any money on it. I already heard about some hotshot sniper who's been coming up here, and I've got a suspicion that he may be right next to me."

Johnny laughed. "All right. Twelve shots and the loser buys beer. How about that?"

"A round of beer I can afford. Do your best. We doing rapid-fire or aim-and-shoot?"

"Either one is fine by me. You pick."

Bobby waited for the signal to stop shooting, then he changed the targets, returned and got in position. "If it's all the same to you, I'll go with aim-and-shoot."

Bobby took his time with each shot, and when he finished, they checked the target with the binoculars. "Looks like six out of twelve in center. None dead center."

He handed the glasses to Johnny. "Here, you can check."

"No need to," Johnny said, then he lay down to take his shots. He did six aim-and-shoot, and did rapid-fire for the next six. When they checked with the glasses, Bobby shook his head and whistled. "I haven't seen shooting like that since the competition came here ten years ago. You got ten center shots, and it looks like three, maybe four of them are dead center. Pretty impressive shit."

"Thanks," Johnny said.

"Looks like I'm buying," Bobby said. "Wanna stop at Lily's place?"

"Sounds good to me," Johnny said. "I remember my old man always said they had good, cold beer."

"The way my old man used to tell it, the only good beer *was* a cold beer."

They both laughed, then Bobby said. "All right, see you there in fifteen. You remember how to get there."

"Know the route like the back of my hand," Johnny said. "Let me check out, and I'll be right behind you."

It took about ten or fifteen minutes to get to Lily's, and as soon as Johnny pulled into the parking lot, it brought back memories. They weren't good memories, but not many of his were. He parked and went inside. Bobby was already sitting at a table near the far corner and had a pitcher of beer in front of him. A frosted mug awaited Johnny as he sat.

"Good thing I remembered how to get here," Johnny said. "I wouldn't want this mug to get warm."

"They've always got cold ones," Bobby said as he filled Johnny's mug. "So tell me how you got to be such a damn good shot. I know you were good as a kid, but damn . . . what I saw you do today was unbelievable."

Johnny's face got red, as if he were embarrassed. "I'll give you the short story," he said "I joined the Marines to get the hell out of Cleveland, and when they saw my shooting, they pushed me toward sniper school. I ended up going to their sniper training in Quantico, VA and after that, to assignments overseas."

"So how did you end up back in Cleveland?"

Johnny laughed. "After going through so much trouble to get out of here, I decided I wanted to return and be a cop here."

Bobby set his mug down hard. "Are you shitting me? I'm a damn cop too."

"Get the hell out of here," Johnny said.

"No kidding. I just moved into Homicide about a year ago."

"No shit!" Johnny said. "That's where I want to go eventually, but I'm on patrol now."

"Which district they put you in?"

"I'm on the east side with the Fighting Fourth."

"Damn, sorry to hear that," Bobby said. "I don't wish that assignment on the people I *don't* like."

"No shit about that," Johnny said. "When my wife asked me where I'd be stationed, I didn't know whether to say the Fourth District or the east jungle. And she's having a fit about it. She's pregnant with our second kid, and she gets worried easy."

"She's got a right to be worried," Bobby said. "My wife would be worried, and she's not pregnant."

Johnny signaled the waitress for another round. "This round is on me," he said.

"I'll tell you what," Bobby said. "I'll ask around and see if there's not a better assignment for you."

"No, don't do that," Johnny said. "I appreciate the gesture, and I'd love to get out of there, but I don't want it to look like somebody pulled strings for me."

The waitress brought the beer and another basket of pretzels and nuts and set them on the table. "Here you go, boys. Holler if you need anything else."

"If you're sure about that, fine," Bobby said. "But if you change your mind, let me know."

"I'll tell you what you *can* do for me," Johnny said. "You remember those targets my old man used to buy from PJ?"

Bobby leaned close to Johnny. "You mean the ones of black people?"

"Yeah, the ones showing the whole body and where it looked as if the heart was beating. And *center* of course, was the heart."

"Yeah, he might still have some in the basement," Bobby said. "Not much demand for them anymore though."

"If you could get me some, I'd appreciate it," Johnny said. "I've looked a few other places, but I can't find any. Found a couple *really* old ones with that ayatollah guy from Iran, and I found some newer ones that featured Bin Laden and other sand niggers, but nothing like what your dad had."

Bobby looked around. "Be careful what you say, Johnny. Not everybody agrees with how we think. Even around here, they don't."

Johnny shrugged. "You're probably right. I'll watch what I say."

"In the meantime, I'll see what I can do," Bobby said. "I can probably scrape some up. If you're gonna use 'em at the range though, I'd make sure there aren't too many people around. Especially with this shit we've had going on with that guy killing black girls."

"What? He's only got one or two, right?"

Bobby shook his head. "No, this has been going on for about five or six years. Maybe longer. I think he's gotten seven or eight. The weird thing is, he starts and stops. He'll kill a few, then the shootings stop, then a couple years later, he'll kill a few more."

"Bullshit," Johnny said. "It's probably somebody copying him, that's all."

"Not from what I heard," Bobby said. "The word is, it's the same guy."

Johnny slugged the remainder of his beer. "And you know this how?"

"Got a buddy on the team looking into it. In fact, I might get on the team myself."

Johnny nudged his shoulder. "Get out. For real?"

"Nothing's guaranteed, but I think it's gonna happen."

"Do you *want* on it? Why?"

"Overtime, my man. Whenever this guy cranks up, the overtime for people on the task force is handed out like candy. And I don't mean overtime where you actually have to work for it. I mean sitting in the bar drinking and bullshitting."

"Damn! I could use some of that, especially with a new kid coming soon."

"I definitely can't get you on the case because you need to be Homicide, but if this guy cranks up the killings, I'll bet the captain makes a new joint task force. If that happens, maybe my buddy can pull a few strings."

"Let me know," Johnny said. "I wouldn't mind a few strings being pulled for that."

"All right," Bobby said as he stood. "But I've got to go. See you around."

Johnny stretched his hand out. "Yeah, see ya Bobby. I'm glad we caught up after all this time. And say hi to your dad. I always like PJ."

SOMETHING ROTTEN IN CPD

Johnny walked in the door wearing a frown, though it disappeared with Michele's kiss. He returned the kiss, then patted her stomach lightly. "How's my little boy doing?"

"First, you have no idea if it's a boy or girl, and second, that is a sour look on your face. What's wrong?"

"Nothing and everything," Johnny said.

Michele smiled as she handed Johnny a beer. "I speak three languages, but you're going to have to explain that one to me."

Johnny laughed and pulled her onto his lap. "*Nothing* because I'm married to the sexiest, most beautiful, sweetest woman in the world."

"And *everything*?" Michele asked.

"*Everything* because I just spent a few hours with the most disgusting racist piece of shit you've ever seen. And he's with the department."

Michele sat up and stared. "With the department, as in he's a cop?"

"Not just a cop," Johnny said. "He's with Homicide."

"Oh, my God! What are you going to do about it? Are you going to tell the captain?"

"I'm thinking I might use Bobby as a means to get in with that type of person. If Bobby is like that, and he's in Homicide, I'm guessing there are more like him sprinkled throughout the department. Robbery, patrol, special crimes. Hell, maybe even personnel and IA. I wouldn't think so, but you never can tell."

"And you think he can help you find this serial killer? How? What's somebody like him going to do?"

"For one, he's got a lot of connections in Homicide, and one of them is on the serial killer case. Secondly, he's just the type of ass who will know people similar to whoever's doing this. I wouldn't be surprised if the killer is a friend of his."

"You can't think that?" Michele asked.

"I *do* think that," Johnny said. "I already laid the groundworks, pretending to be a racist myself."

"Johnny, nobody will believe that," Michele said.

"I think they might. The last anyone remembers, I was Michael McCoy's kid who was learning to shoot. And my father was as racist as they come. It wouldn't be a stretch for them to think I followed in his footsteps."

She kissed my cheek and stood. "If you're done being a bigot and racist for the day, how about an omelet for dinner?"

"An omelet sounds great," Johnny said. "You know I love your omelets."

"Bacon, eggs, tomatoes, cheese, and onions?"

"Don't forget mushrooms," Johnny said.

"God, you're spoiled," Michele said. "But sit tight, and I'll have it ready in about ten minutes. I need to do them separate because Chloe doesn't like onions."

In the morning, Johnny got in early and left a note on Margie's desk, asking her to call him. Twenty minutes later, she rang. "Johnny McCoy."

"Johnny, this is Margie. You wanted me to call?"

Johnny lowered his voice to almost a whisper. "Margie, this is probably not a good time to talk. There are a lot of people around."

"Aren't they all cops?" Margie asked.

"They are," Johnny said, "and that may be the problem. Ask the captain if it's possible to meet somewhere away from the station. I don't want to sound like I'm dreaming up conspiracies, but there are things going on that aren't right. Can you ask him, Margie?"

Margie sighed. "I'll ask, but Captain Helger is a busy man. I'll call you back when I hear."

"How about I call you back in a few hours? You think you'll know by then?"

"I should know in less than an hour. Why? What's going on, Johnny?"

"Margie, I can't trust the people around me. I'll explain when I meet the captain. Ask him if he can meet at Dom's coffee shop on the north side of the Fourth District. If he can meet, just tell me the time, and I'll make it."

Johnny met Captain Helger at one, just after lunch. Helger sat with his back facing the street, but didn't seem surprised when Johnny approached. "This needs to be good, McCoy. I canceled two meetings to come here."

"I think it is, sir. I suspect there are some cops in the department with racist views and attitudes. We can't afford to have that, especially with this killer on the loose. If the public or the media got hold of information like that, they'd have a field day with it. Can you imagine the outrage if people thought we had racist cops on the task force and we weren't able to solve the case of the serial killer who is shooting black women."

"And what makes you think there are racists in the department?"

"I've been going to all the top shooting ranges, Captain. While I'm shooting, I've been pretending to be a racist myself. On one occasion, I even had a homicide cop approach me. And I guarantee you, he wasn't faking."

"A Homicide cop? Who?"

"I'd rather not say yet," Johnny said. "Let me look into it a little more. I intend to frequent these ranges for a while, especially before the contest. Maybe by then, I'll have more to go on."

"Are you saying you think somebody at these ranges may be the shooter of these black women?"

"I won't swear to it, Captain. And I'm *not* saying it's a cop. But that's one of the reasons I want to look into this further. If I get anything definitive, I'll let you know."

Captain Helger handed Johnny a card. "This has my cell phone on it. Call me directly if you get anything."

Johnny took the card and put it in his pocket. "Will do, Captain. I'll keep you posted on what I find out."

As Johnny walked out, the captain said, "And don't forget about that contest. Margie is getting a lot of interest from all over. I think we're going to have a lot of people show up at this event."

"Let's hope so," Johnny said.

A SURREPTITIOUS MEETING

Bobby sat around the table with four other guys, all cops. "I'm telling you," he said. "McCoy might be a real candidate. I was at the range with him the other day, and he was 'nigger' this and 'sand nigger' that. Ain't no way that kid's a plant."

"It seems odd that he shows up all of a sudden like this and he's spewing off that kind of language," Milt said. "I'd think a new person would watch their mouth around people they don't know."

Bobby looked over to Milt. "You wouldn't say that if you knew his father. He was the most racist son of a bitch I ever saw. He used to drag Johnny to the shooting range every week and browbeat him until he hit center with his shots. And this was when the kid was ten years old. I'm telling you, if the kid didn't get three out of four of his shots in the center, his old man would beat him when he got home."

"I don't know if I feel comfortable letting him in just yet," Pete said. "One mistake and we're all toast. I've got a pension to think of."

"A pension? Pete, you're barely thirty years old. You're a long ways off from a pension," Bobby said.

Milt laughed. "You better get your ED fixed first, before your wife runs off with the mailman or something. Then your pension won't matter because she'll take that too."

"Screw you," Pete said.

"Not gonna happen," Milt said. "Ain't nobody traveling down the Hershey highway on me. Not while I'm still breathing anyway."

Spence laughed so hard he almost spat his beer out. "The Hershey highway? Good one. I hadn't heard that before."

"All right, let's do this," Pete said. "For the next couple weeks, we'll watch him and see if we pick anything up. After that time, if all still seems good, we'll invite him for a beer one night and see what we think."

Everyone lifted their mugs and tapped them. "Good idea," Milt said. "I'm for it."

"Sounds good to me," Bobby and Spence both said.

For the next two weeks, Johnny had a tail everywhere he went: the shooting ranges, the coffee shops, lunch spots, even when he took Michele and Chloe to the movies. And when the tails weren't obvious, they were in the open, like when he'd *accidentally* meet Bobby at Max's range. They'd usually end up at Lily's after shooting, and there would almost always be one of Bobby's other friends there, though they'd remain unnoticed and unseen. Johnny didn't know Spence, Pete, or Milt, so he had no reason to recognize them, but they were there—listening and watching.

~

Late on a Wednesday night, Bobby and the other three got together. "Before we discuss anything else, anybody got anything on McCoy?" Bobby asked.

"I do," Pete said. "It may be nothing, but it may not."

"Spit it out," Milt said.

"I followed him to a small coffee shop near the Fourth District just after lunch today."

"Odd choice for coffee, but go on. He works over there, so that might explain it," Bobby said.

"That's not what's odd," Pete said. "He was in there about twenty minutes, then he came out and left. I waited a minute before I followed, and while I'm waiting, guess who exits the same coffee shop? Captain Helger."

"Are you sure it was Helger?" Spence asked.

"Spence, I know a damn captain's uniform when I see one, and I sure as shit know what Helger looks like."

"Did he see you?" Milt asked.

Pete shook his head. "No way. As soon as I laid eyes on him, I ducked so he couldn't see me, and I didn't get up till he left."

"What the hell?" Milt asked. "Why would McCoy be meeting with the captain all the way over in the Fourth? I can understand why Johnny might be there, but not the captain. And if they're going to so much trouble to meet, it's got to be something on the sly."

Bobby nodded. "I agree. And I don't like it. We need to get eyes on him during the day. We know anyone who works with him?"

"I don't know anyone who works with him, but you'll probably see him at the range tomorrow or the next day, Bobby. See what you can find out," Spence said.

～

Bobby ran into Johnny at Max's range two days later. Johnny was shooting the long-range shots, and he had that part of the range to himself. Bobby walked up and sat next to him, waiting for Johnny to finish shooting.

"You must have scared everyone away," he said. "I haven't seen it this empty for months."

"Must be a slow day, is all," Johnny said. "What's up? You shooting? I don't see a gun."

"Thought about it, but then I checked my wallet and decided I better not."

Johnny laughed. "I know what you mean there. It gets damn expensive if you do this often. I'm already catching hell from my wife. She's telling me all the money I'm wasting here could be used for baby clothes."

Bobby joined Johnny in laughing. "You know she's right, don't you? This is a waste of money, not to mention time."

Johnny began packing things up to leave, and he talked to Bobby as he did, but he lowered his voice. "Ordinarily, I'd agree with you, but there is a method to my madness."

"Really? And what's that?"

"The captain asked me to be on the shooting team for this upcoming contest. He must have seen the sniper school on my record."

"What? There's a prize or something?" Bobby asked.

Johnny shook his head. "No prize, but I've placed a bunch of bets that I'll win. In most cases, I even got odds. So if I win this thing, I'll haul in a boatload of cash."

"Are you sure you're on the team? Did Helger tell you for sure?"

"He did," Johnny said. "In fact, he asked me to meet him at an out-of-the-way cafe near my beat in the Fourth. I met him there a couple of days ago, in fact."

"Damn, Johnny, that's great. I hope he doesn't go back on his word."

Johnny picked up his gun and binoculars and walked inside to checkout. "I'll tell you what, Bobby. If the son of a bitch reneges on this, I'll shoot for the other side. One way or another, I plan on collecting that money. My bets were on *me* winning. It doesn't matter which team I'm on."

Bobby slapped Johnny on the back. "That's the spirit, Johnny. Get it any way you can. In fact, now that I know about it, I'm gonna put a few bucks down on you too. Might just earn myself some green."

Bobby opened the door to go outside and Johnny said, "Hey, Bobby. Where ya going? How about a beer or two at Lily's?"

"I can't," Bobby said. "Promised the old lady I'd be home early. Maybe next time."

"All right, see ya then," Johnny said.

When Johnny got home, Michele greeted him with a kiss and a smile. "Had my first checkup today, and things went great. The doctor said everything looked good."

Johnny kissed her and held her close. "I'm excited, babe. Nothing could be better news."

"How about your day? How did it go?"

"Great. I think I dodged a bullet too."

"In what way?" Michele asked. "Tell me about it."

"I met the captain the other day at a coffee shop near the Fourth, and when I was leaving, I thought I saw a cop I'd seen around a few times. I don't know him, but I've seen him. Anyway, I drove a couple blocks, then turned and came behind him. He was still sitting there, and when Helger came out of the coffee shop, the guy ducked as if he didn't want to be seen."

"That doesn't make sense, Johnny. Why would someone be following you? Even if it isn't you, why would they be following the captain?"

Johnny shook his head. "I don't know, Michele. But I think I'll have to be a lot more careful."

"One thing is for sure," Michele said. "If you think someone followed you, the meeting place needs to be moved. And you need to figure out how someone knew about this."

"I agree," Johnny said. "I'll give it some thought tonight."

A NEW MEETING PLACE

On his way to work, Johnny called the captain's cell phone.

"Helger," he answered.

"Captain, this is Johnny McCoy."

"What is it, McCoy? Something wrong?"

"Might be, sir. We were followed to the coffee shop the other day, and it was another cop."

"What? Are you sure about this?"

"Positive, sir. I even turned around and came up behind him, and when he saw you exit the shop, he ducked as if he didn't want to be seen. He watched you pull away, then he waited a few seconds and left."

"Maybe he was following me," Helger said.

"I don't think so, sir. After you left, he waited a few seconds, but then he went the other way. Unless he had a partner to pick up your tail, he wasn't after you."

"And you're sure he was a cop?"

"Definitely, sir. I've seen him around, but I don't know his name."

"Son of a bitch," Helger said. "This is getting serious. I need some time to think about this. Call me tonight, and we'll figure something out."

~

Johnny spent the day on routine patrol, but when it came time to sign off, he headed to the homicide detectives' favorite bar.

Johnny walked in and sat at the bar. "Whatever's on tap," he said, and the bartender filled a mug and placed it in front of him. "New here, ain't ya?"

"Yes and no," Johnny said. "When I was a kid, I spent many a night sitting outside in the car and waiting for my father to come out. He'd always say he was stopping for one drink, then two hours later, he'd emerge looking like he had five and smelling like he had ten."

"Who was your father?"

"Mike McCoy," Johnny said. "He wasn't a very likable sort, but I'm sure he was a good customer."

The bartender nodded. "I remember Mike. Sorry about what happened."

A guy in a light-gray suit walked up and sat next to Johnny and held out his hand. "Mark Angelo," he said. "Did I hear you say you're Mike McCoy's kid?"

"I said it," Johnny said. "Not proudly, but I said it."

"What brings you down here? Don't tell me you got the bug?"

"If by 'got the bug' you mean, did I fall to the lure of being one of Cleveland's finest—yeah, I did. My wife doesn't like it. My relatives don't like it. And there are more days than not, *I* don't like it. But I guess that's in the past now."

"Where you working?" Mark asked.

"Fourth District," Johnny said.

Angelo whistled. "The Fighting Fourth. I knew a lot of people who served over there." He laughed then. "Not many of them still alive though."

Johnny took a long sip of his beer. "Ain't that the truth. Tough place, the Fourth is."

"Tough ain't the word. I told my wife that the Fourth is where we should be training our soldiers for fighting. Let 'em have some *real* experience with guerrilla warfare."

Johnny laughed at that and slapped Angelo on the back. "You've got that right. I spent four years with the Marines, and I can say the Fourth would be as good a training ground as boot camp."

"So what brings you down here?" Angelo asked.

"To tell you the truth," Johnny said, "I've been intrigued by this serial killer case. I mean, I don't know much about it, but from what I've read and the little bit I've heard, it's one for the books. I mean a guy killing, then stopping, then starting up again. It's unusual, isn't it?"

Angelo looked over his shoulder, then the other way. "They've got everyone on a tight leash regarding this, but I can tell you that they've got all task members busting their asses. The problem is, we don't have enough to go on."

Johnny spun his stool around so he faced Angelo. "You mean, you're on the case?"

He nodded. "Been on it for almost two years. They brought me in to try to help solve it because my conviction rate was so high. But I haven't been able to do shit. And it's not for lack of trying."

"Damn, I'd cut off my left nut to get on that case."

"Why are you so interested?"

"I love this city. I know that sounds corny, but I do. And I hate to see the city get a bad name. The longer crap like this goes on, the worse it makes Cleveland look. It's why I became a cop."

Angelo ordered another round, then leaned in close. "I'll tell you what, kid. The word is they're going to re-organize this task force. If they do, I'll see if I can slip your name in as a recommendation. How's that?"

Johnny perked up. "Are you shitting me? I'd love it. I mean, *love it.*"

Angelo grabbed his drink and stood. "All right. Consider it done. Now I gotta make the rounds. I can't be depriving all these good souls of my company."

"I wouldn't dare do that, Mark. And thanks for the company," Johnny said.

Johnny thought about a lot on his drive home, but mostly he thought about what Angelo said—about the possibility of getting on the task force. *If I could get on that task force, I might be able to get something done.*

As he got on the interstate, he dialed the captain. "Captain Helger, is this a good time to talk?"

"McCoy?"

"Yes, sir. I'm on my way home, so I thought I'd call."

"Let me step outside. I've got a few people over tonight." Helger put the call on hold, then came back on a moment later. "Okay, I'm on the patio now. What's up?"

"I thought we should meet, sir, but not the same place."

"I agree," Helger said. There was a pause, then he asked, "You live on the west side, right?"

"Yes, sir," Johnny said.

"How about if we meet at the Starbucks right off of I–90, by Edgewater?"

"Sounds good to me. Even if someone is following one of us, I can't imagine they'd start from our houses. Let's make it early. How about six-thirty?"

"I can do that," Helger said. "It will be painful, but I can do it."

"See you then, sir."

A SPECIAL REQUEST

Johnny thought he'd have to wait for Helger, but the captain was on time. Johnny nodded to him as he walked in, then Helger ordered coffee and joined Johnny at the table.

"You realize this is an ungodly hour to meet, don't you?"

"I do, sir. But I had to get this out before I lost my nerve."

Helger looked confused. "Get what out? What's on your mind?"

"I want to be on the task force, sir."

"*The* task force. The serial killer task force?"

"That's the one, sir. And I have to confess, that's the reason I suggested the contest. I thought we might use it as a way to draw out the person who's doing this."

Helger looked at him skeptically. "You realize the task force consists of much more experienced men. Most of them are homicide detectives, although we have a few LE personnel from the State Police and the FBI."

"I understand that, sir. And I'm not trying to be pushy, but I feel I can add value to the investigation due to my background with long-range weapons."

Captain Helger sipped on his coffee, then gave a short nod. "Let's see how it goes with the shooting contest. When that's over, I'll make a decision. How's that?"

"It's more than I could ask for, sir. Thanks."

After Helger left, Johnny waited fifteen or twenty minutes before he left. He took a roundabout way to the station also, one that would allow him to spot any tails easier. Despite continual checking, he didn't see anyone. It didn't put him at ease though, it just confirmed his gut feeling that whoever was tailing him wouldn't do it in the morning. *I'll have to check during the day and on the way home.*

He spent the day fighting fires in the Fourth, which meant busting drug dealers, handling domestic disturbances, and seizing guns from kids not old enough to drink. There were a lot of bad places in Cleveland, but the Fourth District had to be the worst.

At the end of the day, Johnny headed toward Max's to practice his shooting. Bobby was pulling out of the parking lot as Johnny pulled in. Johnny came to a stop and rolled down his window. "Hey, asshole. You ducking me? I came here to shoot for beers."

Bobby laughed. "I'm sure you did, Johnny, but I've barely got enough to pay for my own beers. You can join me at Lily's if you want."

Johnny shook his head. "That's all right. I need to get some practice in before this contest. I can't afford to lose."

"You better not, damnit. I've got fifty bucks on you."

"All right," Johnny said. "I better work on making sure that's a good investment. See ya later."

"Yeah, see ya," Bobby said, and pulled onto the road.

Bobby continually checked his rearview mirror, but after a few miles, he relaxed. No one was there. He pulled into Lily's parking lot and went inside. Spence, Pete, and Milt were already there, and from the looks of it, they'd already had a few rounds. "Start early, did we?" Bobby asked.

"No, *we* started on time. But *some* asshole I know is late," Pete said.

Spence signaled the waitress for another round, then Milt began with the questions. "Well, what the hell did you hear? We got us a traitor or what?"

Bobby shook his head as he took his first swig of beer. "I'll have to admit, you had me concerned, but I met up with him at the range. He complained about the cost, and I told him it was a waste of money considering how good he was. Then he confided in me, telling me the captain asked him to be on the shooting team for the upcoming competition, so Johnny wisely placed a few bucks on himself to win. He stands to rake in some good cash."

Pete nodded. "So you think that's why he was meeting with the captain?"

"Pretty damn sure of it," Bobby said. "And to double-check, I went right out and placed a few bucks on him myself."

"What's that got to do with anything?" Milt asked.

"It told me that the bookies already knew he'd be one of the shooters. You know how the damn bookies are; they know the scoop before we do."

"Ain't that the truth," Spence said. "You think I should plunk down a few bucks?"

"If you're gonna do it, it better be quick. He's already down to even money."

"So where's that leave us?" Pete asked.

"I still say we should wait," Milt said. "At least until after the shoot."

"I'll go along with that," Bobby said. "Besides, I don't want anything distracting him beforehand. I told Johnny I put fifty bucks on him, but I really put three hundred."

"Damn, Bobby. You must think he's really good."

"He's better than good, Pete. I've shot against him six times now, and he's kicked my ass each time."

Spence looked side to side, then leaned in close. "All right, enough of the Johnny talk. What are we gonna do about the other?"

"I think the killings have been dormant long enough," Milt said. "It's time to start something new."

"Same process?" Pete asked. "Burn a few crosses, then the killings start?"

"Sounds good to me," Bobby said. "It worked great before."

"Then how about we start near the east side tomorrow night?" Spence asked. "I've got a ten-foot cross ready to go."

"Tomorrow night it is," Bobby said. "Let's start about ten."

"Where are we going to meet?" Pete asked.

"Nothing wrong with meeting here," Bobby said. "We're familiar faces by now, so it won't be out of the ordinary."

"I agree," Milt said. "Let's plan on meeting here at seven."

They held up our mugs and tapped them in salute. "Till then," they said, and chugged them down.

LET ME PICK YOUR BRAIN

Johnny went to the patrolmen's association bar, the one with the Zone-Car "an old police car that people could sit in to drink or do other things. It was usually people who already had *too much* to drink, but sometimes it was just used for private conversations or other private activities." He was looking for Angelo, who wasn't at his normal perch, but when Johnny asked about him, the bartender acknowledged he was around somewhere.

"Angelo's here," he said. "But you'll need to find him before he passes out. Or at the very least, while he can still talk."

Johnny made his way through the bar and finally found Angelo chatting it up with two female officers young enough to be his daughters. "Angelo," he said. "Long time, no see."

Angelo scowled and turned to face Johnny. "You've got a terrible sense of timing, McCoy. I was just about to go home with two sexy broads."

"First off, if you took them home, they'd eat you for breakfast. At best, they might rub against you while they roll you."

Angelo sneered. "Cynical son of a bitch, aren't you? They're cops."

"Even cops take advantage of the weak. I call it realistic, Angelo. Sorry."

Angelo gulped down the rest of his beer and set the empty mug on the counter. "Another one," he said, then turned to me. "So what are you after tonight, pain-in-the-ass?"

"Same thing I was after before—information on the serial killer."

"Shit," Angelo said. "What do you know about it?"

"Other than he's targeting young black girls—nothing."

"Well, it usually starts with crosses being burned, and they're usually burned in a black neighborhood. Sometimes it's just one, sometimes two. But sure as honey's sweet, not long after, the killings ramp up. And the victims have all been shot from long range, so the killer—whoever the fucker is—is a damn good shot. And from what I hear, that puts you on the suspect list, McCoy."

"What type of gun is used? What ammo?" Johnny asked.

"If I told you that, they'd hang me up by the balls and set me on fire. If you get on the task force, you'll be privy to the information, but not before."

"And you won't tell me?"

"I *can't* tell you. It's *need to know only*. And unless you're on the task force, you don't need to know."

I looked over and saw a couple getting out of the back seat of the Lounge Car. At the very least, they'd been making out, at the worst . . .? Let's just say I didn't want to sit in the back seat. "Hey, Angelo, let's grab a seat in the Lounge Car. It's empty."

"Why the hell do I want to do that? You plan on giving me a hand job?"

"No, Angelo, but you're going to tell me more about the serial killer."

We sat in the front seat of the car, and I handed Angelo a full bottle of his favorite Scotch. After half a bottle was consumed, he opened up.

"At first, they said all the shots were from a seven millimeter cartridge, then they said it was a .30 caliber, and the last I heard it was a .338 load. The fact is, I don't know what the hell it is, which is part of the problem, McCoy. It can't be all three. I've never heard of that."

"But it's one of those three?" Johnny asked.

"Hell, I don't know," Angelo said. "I don't actually see the files. Some higher-ups see the files and report down the chain. All I know is it starts with the crosses being burned, and the only reason I know that is because the damn papers report it."

"So who's following whose lead?" Johnny asked. "Are they following your storyline, or are you following theirs?"

Angelo shook his head as he took another swig. "Damned if I know, McCoy. Your guess is as good as mine."

"My guess is it's a bunch of degenerate cops who are off living out their racist fantasies."

"No way," Angelo said. "No way a cop would do this, no matter how racist they were. I mean, I'm not crazy about blacks, but they *are* people. And you can't just kill people."

"I'm glad you think that way, Angelo, but not everybody does."

"Come on, Johnny. You don't believe that, do you?"

"Angelo, when my father was alive, he'd swerve to avoid hitting a squirrel or a rabbit, but not a black person. He was a racist son of a bitch. The worst I've seen."

Angelo put down the bottle and stared. "Are you shitting me? He was that way for real?"

Johnny nodded. "Trust me. It was for real."

Johnny drove home that night, both encouraged and discouraged. Encouraged because he'd made headway with Angelo and gotten him to open up more about the case. Discouraged because he hadn't learned much more than he already knew. One thing was for sure. This was going to take a lot of work.

DO YOU KNOW WHAT YOU'RE DOING?

Johnny spent all morning dealing with issues on the east side, mostly tracking down a group of thugs who had robbed several older women as they walked to the grocery store. The muggers made sure to get them on their way *to* the store, not going home. That way, they'd still have their cash or food stamps or whatever with them. After two or three hours of staking out the stores, Johnny and his partner caught three of the muggers red-handed and hauled them in.

As he did the paperwork at his desk, his phone rang. "Johnny McCoy."

"McCoy, this is Sahrina down in Homicide. Your uncle asked me to call with a message. He asked if you could drop by to see him after two. He's busy until then."

"Are you talking about Uncle Bob, down in personnel?"

"He's the one," Sahrina said.

Johnny went to see Uncle Bob just after two. "He in?" he asked Bob's assistant as he approached.

"He is. And he's expecting you."

Johnny walked in, looking somewhat confused, then Bob got up and closed the door. He poked his head into the hallway and said, "Janice, I don't want to be disturbed." After which, he closed the door and sat. He stared at Johnny and asked, "You being careful enough, boy?"

"Careful with what?" Johnny asked.

"I heard that you were looking into the serial killer case, and people are wondering why. You're not in Homicide, and you're not on the task force. 'So why is he looking into it?' people are asking."

"Who's doing the asking?"

"Can't say who," Bob said. "Just know that it's more than a random cop who's curious. Whatever the hell you're doing is attracting attention."

"I guess that's good and bad," Johnny said.

"I can see all the bad aspects, but I'm having a difficult time visualizing the good ones," Bob said. "Care to enlighten me?"

Johnny thought for a moment, then said, "From what I've heard so far, the people on the team don't know enough."

Bob let out a chuckle. "Do you want to tell me what the hell that means?"

"It means that considering as much evidence as they *should* have gathered by now, they aren't up to speed with what's going on. Don't get me wrong, Uncle Bob. I'm not saying I could do any better, but I doubt if I could do much worse."

"If that's all you've learned from poking around on this case, I'd recommend stopping. What you told me amounts to nothing, and you poking around will definitely get you—and possibly others— in trouble. Remember, you're not supposed to be privy to *anything* regarding this case."

"That's not all, Uncle Bob. You know the upcoming shooting contest, where two CPD officers will take on all comers? I'm going to be one of the shooters for the department."

Bob stood up and shook Johnny's hand. "Congratulations, Johnny. I feel more confident of CPD's chance of winning now that I know you'll be representing us."

"Thanks, Uncle Bob. But what I was getting at, is this will provide me with the opportunity to see a bunch of expert shooters up close. And if I know more about the specifics of the case, it might give me additional insight."

Bob sighed and leaned back in the chair. "Johnny, that's all well and good, but officially, you don't need additional insight. You're not supposed to be looking into this case. In fact, you're not supposed to know *anything* about this case."

"All right, Uncle Bob. Assume from now on, that I'm off the case."

"Off the case! Johnny, you were never *on* the case. And you never will be if you keep this shit up. And as far as your statement, does that mean you'll be careful of who you talk to? Or does it mean you'll stop looking into it? They are quite different statements."

"It means you won't hear any more about me looking into the case," Johnny said.

"You said, 'I won't *hear* any more.' Does that mean you won't *do* any more or just that I won't hear about it?"

Johnny stood and smiled. "Uncle Bob, I appreciate all you've done, but now the rest is up to me."

"I didn't do anything, remember? And if you get caught looking into this, you better remember. It would be my job if the captain finds out I let you see those files. Which brings up another point. If you still have copies of those files, you need to get rid of them. I can't risk you getting caught with copies of those files. If they find them, they won't stop until they discover who you got them from."

"I'm not going to say anything, Uncle Bob. You know that."

"I don't think you would, Johnny. But it wouldn't take much detective work to figure out where you got the files once they go through who had access to them. Your uncle would be a logical choice."

Johnny nodded. "I see what you mean, Uncle Bob, and you're right."

"Does that mean you're going to stop?" Bob asked. "I can't afford to be caught up in something like this."

"All right," Johnny said. "I'll stop. It looks as if the killings have stopped anyway. Haven't had one in a long time."

"I wouldn't say that, Johnny. They've stopped before and for a lot longer, only to start back up again. I need you to promise me you won't go off like a bat out of hell, if they start up again."

Johnny sighed. "I won't, Uncle Bob. I'll try to do this the legitimate way."

"And what way is that?" Bob asked.

"I put in a request for assignment to the task force and ultimately, to Homicide."

"A request? To whom?"

"The captain, and he seemed open to the idea. He said we'd discuss it after the contest."

Bob shook his head as he stood up to show Johnny out. "Let's hope he okays it. If he does, we won't have any trouble."

"Sounds good to me," Johnny said. "Thanks, Uncle Bob."

THE SHOOT

Johnny worked all morning patrolling the streets of the Fourth. Sometime during lunch, he received a call from Margie, Captain Helger's assistant.

"Johnny, the captain asked me to call and tell you to get your ass back to the station, or better yet, go home. He said, and I quote, 'Tell that son of a bitch to get some rest so he's at the top of his game in the morning.'"

"Are you sure?" Johnny asked.

"No, I'm not sure, but the captain is. And he was as serious as I've ever seen him, so if I were you, I'd do what he said, and go home."

Johnny laughed. "I guess you can't argue with the boss."

"You can try," Margie said, "but it won't get you anywhere."

"All right, then. I'm going home," Johnny said.

"Good luck tomorrow," Margie said.

All the way home, Johnny thought about the shoot. He wasn't nervous about his ability to win, but he was anxious about being able to find out anything new. If he was lucky, he'd spot a few new faces, ones he didn't ordinarily see at any of the ranges—if he was lucky. If not, he'd be back to square one, working off the little information he got from the files and what he'd gathered so far from the ranges. Neither one of which was much.

Michele greeted him with a kiss—as usual—then she rubbed her stomach and smiled. "I go for the test in three days, you know. I'm guessing it will be a girl. What about you?"

"A boy, no doubt," he said.

"And what makes you think that?" Michele asked.

"It's in the genes. Almost all my uncles had boys first; in fact, I think all of them did."

"But we had a girl," Michele said.

"I know," Johnny said. "That makes the odds even better for this one to be a boy."

"The only thing that means, is it's time for another girl. The odds are with me."

"With you?"

"Yes, with me. I'm the one rooting for a girl."

"Either way, we should be a tad wealthier by then," Johnny said. "I was able to place quite a bit in bets on the winner of the shooting contest."

Michele laughed. "If that's the case, I think we need to go shopping for a few baby things."

"Hold on a minute," Johnny said. "First, I have to actually win, and second although I'm sure it will be a boy, we should wait for the results of the test just to make sure."

Johnny woke up to the irresistible aroma of bacon cooking. Aside from the smell of coffee brewing, he didn't think there was any other smell as identifiable. At least, no pleasant smell. "I see you're trying to bribe me into those new baby items," he said.

"I wish I had thought of that, but this is because your spoiled daughter insisted on cooking 'Daddy's favorite meal.'"

Johnny walked up behind Chloe and kissed her cheek. "That's my girl. Always taking care of Daddy." He then hugged her and said, "I love you, Chloe."

"I love you too, Daddy. And good luck tonight, but I know you won't need it."

"You're right about that, Chloe. That contest is already won."

Michele turned around and kissed him. "I know that, but I think you still need to convince the judges, so go out there and shoot like hell. Like your life depends on it—because it does."

He sat at the table with Chloe and Michele and ate breakfast, then he drank two cups of coffee. "All right, my lovely wife, I'm off to slay the dragon."

"Good luck," Michele said. "And don't forget to call me as soon as it's over."

"I still wish you'd come," Johnny said. "I'd love to have you there."

"No way," Michele said. "I'm bad luck. If I went and something happened, I'd never forgive myself."

"I'll come, Daddy," Chloe yelled.

Johnny smiled and knelt next to her. "Thank you so much for offering, sweetheart, but you're a little too young for this. When you get older, you can watch Daddy shoot. Okay?"

"Okay, Daddy. But I still wish you good luck."

Johnny roared. "Well, thank you for that. Now, I'm sure I'll win." Johnny kissed Michele goodbye for the third time and then headed for the door. "All right. See you guys tonight."

He got to the range in plenty of time and was greeted by a lot of people he knew. Many of them had placed bets on him as well—or so he heard.

"Go get 'em, Johnny," someone yelled, and when he turned, he saw Bobby standing there with his thumb raised.

"Are you ready?" the captain asked as Johnny passed by.

"Absolutely," he said. "No worries."

The shooting started in ten minutes, so Johnny got his rifle and ammo and took his position with his fellow CPD shooter, a guy named Manny, who had also been in the Marines, but not sniper school.

"You ready?" Manny asked.

"Ready as I can be," Johnny said. "I'm looking forward to a tough shoot. We're up against some pretty good shots."

"I feel comfortable," Manny said. "And I've heard about your shooting."

"We'll see," Johnny said. "Soon enough, we'll see."

The shorter-range rounds went much as Johnny had expected, with both sides racking up excellent scores. CPD had an edge, but only a slight one. Now came the real test though—the five-hundred-yard range. It was the one that separated the men from the boys, as they said.

The competition went first. A guy named Jones from the north side of Cleveland. He took six shots with aim-and-shoot and six more rapid-fire, which were the rules set by the range. Within fifteen seconds, his results came in:

Aim-and-shoot - three center, three near-miss. None dead center.
Rapid-fire - two center, three near-miss, and one miss. None dead center.

An older man from the far east side shot next. He looked to be sixty or seventy, but he moved spryly. He lay down and took very little time aiming. His results came back quickly.

Aim-and-shoot - three center, two near-miss. One dead center.
Rapid-fire - three center, two near-miss. One dead center.

Manny turned to me and raised his eyebrows. "Not bad. I hope I can do as well."

"You will," Johnny said, but he quietly hoped the same.

A youngster from center city shot third. He didn't look to be more than mid-twenties. He plopped down, picked up his rifle, took aim, and shot. He stuffed his mouth with chewing tobacco while everyone waited on results.

Aim-and-shoot - two center, two near-miss. Two dead center.
Rapid-fire - two center, two near-miss, and one miss. One dead center.

Manny tapped Johnny on the arm. "How many shooters have they got?"

"Just one more," Johnny said. "And I heard he's good."

A tall, lanky man who was as thin as a beanstalk approached slowly. He moved with determination and focus. He reminded Johnny of his days in the Marines and how they taught you to breathe slowly and focus.

The guy got in position and took his time. When he finished, he stood, lit a cigarette, and moved aside. There was a confidence in how he moved that spoke volumes.

When the results came back, his confidence proved to be warranted.

Aim-and-shoot - four center, one near-miss. One dead center.
Rapid-fire - three center, two near-miss. One dead center.

"Son of a bitch," Manny said. "He's good."

"You're up next, Manny, and you're good too. Just remember to stay calm."

Manny nodded. "Got it."

Manny got in position, took his time, and fired. His results returned quickly.

Aim-and-shoot - three center, three near-miss. None dead center.
Rapid-fire - three center, two near-miss, and one miss. None dead center.

"Good shooting," Johnny said. "That puts us in the running."

"Only if you can do better than that guy who looked like Abe Lincoln," Manny said. "It's gonna be tough."

Johnny took his time preparing, then when ready, he closed his eyes and breathed slowly. He focused on the target and fired. When he finished the aim-and-shoot, he again breathed slowly and focused, then he did the rapid-fire. Afterward, he stood and waited for the results. He was nervous, but not overly so. The results came back in a flash.

Aim-and-shoot - four center. Two dead center.
Rapid-fire - three center. Three dead center.

When the results were read, people gathered around him, offering congratulations. They had to wait for the official scoring, but it was obvious that CPD had won. Johnny had made it so it wasn't even a contest.

"Damn, but that was some shooting," Bobby said as he walked up to Johnny. "I'm happy as hell for you, but even more so for myself. I had a lot of money riding on your shooting."

Johnny shook Bobby's hand and smiled. "I had more than a few bucks myself," he said. "And that is definitely going to make my wife happy." Johnny stopped as if he just remembered something. "Shit, Bobby, that reminds me. I've got to call her."

He dialed the phone and was greeted by, "Well?"

"You are speaking to the champion shooter of the CPD," Johnny said.

"Oh, my God! Really? I knew you could do it. Congratulations, Johnny."

"Thanks, and before you ask, yes, I know it means I owe you a shopping trip. Give me time to collect, and we'll plan a trip next week."

"Great," Michele said. "We can do it after we get the test results."

THE CROSS

Bobby sat across the table from Pete. "Where the hell are the others?" He asked. "They should have been here ten minutes ago."

"Take it easy, Bobby. Ten minutes is no big deal. They might be stuck in traffic."

Bobby ordered another pitcher of beer and had just poured himself a glass when Spence and Milt walked in. He looked up and shook his head. "About time you got here. I was starting to get concerned."

Pete laughed. "Don't let him bullshit you. He was far past 'starting to get concerned.' He was on the verge of sending out a search party."

"And I believe you," Milt said. "I've seen him when he gets that way. God help the guy who brings his daughter home late from a date."

"Everything ready?" Bobby asked Milt and Spence.

"We've got it in the back of the van," Milt said. "We only used a seven-foot cross, but it's wrapped in rags which are soaked in gasoline. And we've got a garbage can loaded with damn heavy rocks to set the cross in."

"You sure they'll hold it up?" Bobby asked.

"Already tested it," Spence said. "We need to place the cross in first, then set the rocks around the base of it. But it'll hold up great."

"What about the gasoline?" Pete asked. "Won't that fuck up the van?"

"We've got the windows open," Spence said. "And the cross is laid on top of plastic, so the gas won't soak into the carpet. It might take a day or two for the odor to go away, but it'll be fine."

"Okay, are we ready?" Milt asked.

"Not yet," Bobby said. "It's not dark yet. We probably need to give it at least another hour."

Bobby and the rest of them sat around drinking and talking for another hour, then they settled the tab and left. "We should go in one car," Bobby said. "We can park my car in the Starbucks' parking lot heading west on the interstate, and you guys can drop me off on the way home."

"Hop in," Milt said. "Pick your poison—gas smell or worse gas smell. But whichever one you pick, there is a strict no-smoking policy."

"No shit on that," Pete said. "And since Bobby hasn't chosen, I'll take the 'gas smell' as opposed to the 'worse gas smell.' "

"Just get in, asshole, and stop whining. We need to get this over with, and we need to do it sooner rather than later."

"True that," Spence said. "It's about time some more folks died around here. Every time I read the statistics, the city is losing white people and getting darker."

"Yeah," Milt said, "And it's not just spooks. It's Puerto Ricans and Muslims too."

"Let's show them all that they're not welcome in Cleveland," Bobby said.

Milt drove, adhering to the speed limit the whole way. The last thing they wanted was a patrolman pulling them over while they had a cross wrapped in gasoline-soaked rags in the back.

Within twenty minutes, Milt pulled up to the corner they had selected. It was outside one of the busier bodegas on the east side, and it was a heavily populated black part of the city. Best of all, at this time of night, everything was closed—other than the liquor store a block away. They had no concerns though. Even if it had surveillance that worked, it couldn't pick them up from this far away, and they wouldn't be driving past the store on the way out.

Milt pulled the van close to the curb, then Pete and Spence jumped out, hauling the can with them. Johnny took the cross from the back and put it into the can, holding it while they fixed the rocks around the base.

"Hurry up. I can't stand here holding this damn thing. If anyone sees me, I'll be the target."

They fidgeted for another ten seconds, then Milt announced it was ready. "Should be good," he said. "Let go of it, Bobby, and we'll see if it stands on its own."

Bobby carefully let go of the cross, and it stood straight. "Okay, let's hit it," he said.

They jumped in the van, then Spence tossed a lit match into the can. A big *whooshing* sound indicated success, as did the flames soaring into the air.

Milt hit the gas and sped from the scene. "Goddamn, but that went up," he said.

"Like a damn Roman candle," Pete said, and laughed.

"You just need to focus, Milt. The last thing we need is to be stopped. And this is going to draw a lot of attention."

"I hope it does, Bobby. It was a lot of work to get it right," Spence said.

"I'd call the papers and report it, but I don't want them tracing my cell phone," Pete said. "And I don't even know if they have phone booths anymore."

"That'd be worse," Milt said. "If somebody sees you in a phone booth, you'll either be tagged as Superman or a drug dealer."

Bobby laughed. "Just get your ass to Starbucks so I can go home," he said. "And everyone better get some sleep because the shit is gonna hit the fan tomorrow."

"I'd love to be there when the captain hears about it," Pete said.

"Don't worry," Spence said, "if you're anywhere in the building, I'm sure you'll hear him. He's gonna have a cow."

Milt turned on the blinker and slowed enough to turn into the parking lot. "Here you go, Bobby. Drive safely and sleep tight."

"Screw you," Bobby said. "See you in the morning."

WITH GOOD NEWS COMES BAD

Johnny woke up so happy, he almost bounced out of bed. He rushed through brushing his teeth and shaving, then he went to the kitchen. "And how are my two favorite girls this morning? And by that, I mean my beautiful daughter and my slightly wealthier wife?"

"Not as good as you'd think," Michele said.

Johnny rushed over, concern painted on his face. "Why? What's the matter? You feel okay?"

Michele handed him the paper. The headlines seemed to blare at him.

Cross Burnt on East Side in Predominantly Black Neighborhood.

The article went on to mention that:

This isn't the first time a cross has been burned in a black neighborhood. It isn't even the first time in recent years.

And it's not a good omen for the black community. Each time a cross was burned in the past few years, the event was a precursor to the killings of young black women. These killings were the undisputed result of a serial killer who appears to be stalking and killing black women and girls between the ages of thirteen and the mid-twenties.

If the past is a predictor of what is to come, more killings should be expected within days. If that happens, one wonders how long the black community will put up with it. There is almost surely going to be an explosion of some sort.

Johnny read the article, shaking his head the whole time. "You know this is going to interfere with our shopping plans, don't you?"

"If you mean, you'll be working late, I assumed that. Just do whatever you can to get this maniac. And by all means, stay safe."

Johnny gulped the rest of his coffee, then stood. He kissed Michele and Chloe, patted his wife on the butt, then said, "I'm sorry, but I need to go. I know it's going to be nuts down there this morning. And I don't mean a good 'nuts' either."

Johnny got to work a little early, and much as he expected, things were hectic. There were more lieutenants running around than he had ever seen, and all of them seemed to be issuing orders at once. Most of those orders sounded like half the force would be deployed to the east side to prevent any violent breakouts.

He was gathering things to take to work when a call came in from Margie. "He wants to see you now. And from the sounds of his mood, I wouldn't disappoint."

"I'll be right up," Johnny said.

Johnny walked into Captain Helger's office and stood at attention. "You wanted to see me, sir?"

Helger gestured toward a chair, indicating Johnny should sit. "You asked before about being on this task force. Now is your chance. You still want it?"

Johnny perked up, not believing his fortune. "Absolutely, sir. More than anything."

"Keep in mind, I can't just promote you to Homicide, but I can make a special assignment and put you on the task force. I can make excuses due to your expertise with long-range shooting—which no one could deny now. By the way, great shooting. I haven't seen anyone that good."

"Thank you, sir," Johnny said. "What is it you'd want me to do on the task force?"

"First, I want you to pretend as if all was normal. Don't tell anyone you're on the task force. I want you to poke around and see if you can find out anything. Can you do that? Do you have a problem with it?"

"Not at all, sir. I can start today."

"Good," the captain said. "Then get out there and keep your eyes and ears open. Report anything suspicious to me, but go through Margie. If you have to speak to me directly, call my cell phone at night. We'll figure out someplace to meet. And, McCoy, I want a report at the end of each day. I don't care if it goes through Margie or if you have to call me at night, but get it done one way or another."

"Yes, sir," Johnny said, and though he didn't salute, he sounded as if he would. He then left the captain's office and headed for the east side.

"About time you got here," his partner, Bruce, said.

"Sorry about that, Bruce. Helger caught me, and I had to go through a round of bullshit regarding congratulations on the shooting yesterday."

"Oh, damn, I almost forgot about that. Congratulations, man. That was some phenomenal shooting. I heard no one else was close."

"Not quite true," Johnny said. "One guy was damn close. I was nervous as hell after he shot, not knowing if I could even equal his shots."

"But you did, and that's all that matters," Bruce said. "We showed those hillbilly motherfuckers who's the top dog around here."

Johnny laughed. "I don't know if that's what it was all about, Bruce, but if it was, yeah, we showed 'em."

Johnny spent the remainder of the day working with Bruce to contain any problems, but he made note to pay particular attention to the behavior of the other officers—were they shocked, how did they interact with and treat the blacks, and, in general, how shocked were they by what happened. Most officers, even the ones who weren't fond of blacks, were more than surprised. And the majority of them seemed intent on catching whoever did this.

Sometime around noon, he ran into Bobby and his partner, Spence. "Some bunch of shit, huh?" Bobby asked.

Johnny still held suspicion on Bobby, so he looked around, then leaned in and whispered. "I don't know why they stopped at a cross. It would have been a lot better if there was a body attached —a black body."

Bobby looked nervous and glanced left and right. "Johnny, keep it down. You can't talk like that. Now of all times, you can't. If somebody other than me hears you, your ass is fried."

"All right. All right. Just saying. When was the last time you saw this many cops on the east side? Shit, somebody could be robbing a bank across town and nobody would know. What's that all about?"

"It's the way the world works," Bobby said. "Get used to it because I don't see it changing anytime soon."

"I hear ya," Johnny said, "but I didn't join the force for this shit."

"Then why did you join the force? What did you think you'd be doing?"

"I thought I'd be doing real police work. Solving real crimes. How many goddamn Muslims are out there plotting against the government right now? And how many blacks are planning how to overthrow the whites? Those are the sons of bitches we should be after, not somebody who kills a few breeders."

Bobby glanced about again, then placed his hand on Johnny's shoulder. "Whoa, buddy. Take a long breath and calm down. Maybe you should meet with me and a few of my buddies this weekend. How about Friday night at Lily's? Say six o'clock?"

Johnny looked at him and shook his head. "What the hell do I want to meet with your buddies for? They gonna try to talk me out of my ideas?"

"No, nothing like that. Just meet, okay? I promise it won't be a waste of time."

Johnny thought for a moment, then nodded. "Okay, I'll be there, but it better be good."

"Don't worry," Bobby said. "You'll enjoy it."

THE MEET

On Friday night, Johnny made sure he was about ten minutes late. He didn't want to appear too eager. When he walked in the door, Bobby stood and hollered from across the room. "Johnny, over here."

Johnny pulled a chair from another table and sat next to Bobby, between him and the guy Bobby introduced as Pete. "Sorry I'm late," he said. "Had the normal shit to deal with in the Fourth, only now it's times ten since that cross-burning shit.

"Yeah, what kind of an asshole does shit like that?" Spence asked.

"I'm not worried about the asshole who did it, but he could have had the decency to do it somewhere else. For God's sake, I gotta work down there with them JBs."

"JBs?" Milt asked.

Johnny laughed. "Yeah, you know, jungle bunnies."

Spence laughed, as did Pete and Bobby. "Hey, work in the Fourth long enough and you'll know exactly what I mean."

"That bad, huh?" Milt asked.

Johnny shook his head. "Milt, you don't know the half of it. Damn people down there are disgusting. Makes you want to . . ."

"Want to what?" Milt asked.

"I don't know. Sometimes it makes me picture what whoever the hell is doing these killings must feel like."

"Goddamn, Johnny. That's one helluva thing to say," Bobby said.

"Well, I'm sorry, but it does. When I was in the Middle East, my first assignment was to take out one of the insurgents near our territory who was causing trouble." Johnny turned to Bobby and whispered, "Are we among friends?"

Bobby said, "Yeah, you can say anything."

Johnny continued with his story. "So on my first assignment, they told me to take out some guy the minute I saw him. I sat in position for almost two hours, then he showed up. I sighted him in, fixed him in my sights, then I hit him. I hit him in the head, and I swear to God, it reminded me of a watermelon exploding. Like when you hit one with a hammer or something."

Johnny laughed hard. "I don't mean to laugh, but that's what it reminded me of, and I can't get that picture out of my mind. Every time I shoot somebody, I think of an exploding watermelon."

"Every time you shoot somebody? Damn, Johnny. How many people do you shoot?" Pete asked.

"Not as many as I used to," Johnny said. "And surely not as many as deserve it."

Bobby ordered another round for everyone. "This round is on me. Thanks to Johnny's good shooting, I raked in the cash on that contest."

When the beer arrived, everyone raised their mugs and saluted Johnny. "To the sharpest sharp-shooter I know," Bobby said, and they all cheered.

Johnny bought the next round, and when they finished that, they all left, promising to do it again soon.

Michele was waiting for him when he walked in, and she wore a smile a mile wide.

"I know. I know," he said. "I missed the appointment, but I warned you it might happen. Are you upset?"

"I assumed you'd miss the appointment, considering what has been going on. Besides, how could I be upset about anything when I'm going to have a new baby girl."

Johnny picked her up and hugged her. "A girl! Hot dog. I know you're happy now."

"And you're not?"

"Of course, I am. How can you even ask that. I may have wished for a boy, but any child that's half you will be almost perfect. Besides, now we'll have two perfect girls like Chloe." Johnny looked around. "Where is she, by the way? Did you tell her?"

"Sorry, I did. But I had to. She was pestering me to death."

"How did she know you'd find out today?" Johnny asked.

"I think she must have overheard us talking. I know it doesn't seem like it, but they understand a lot more than we think at that age."

"Don't worry about me," Johnny said. "I just wanted to know how she felt about having competition."

Michele kissed him. "I don't think she ever worries about that. She has you wrapped around her finger, and she knows it. But thanks, Johnny. I love you."

She grabbed Johnny's hand and led him to the sofa. "Now sit down and tell me how your day went. I know it couldn't have been good."

He shook his head. "It wasn't. The entire east side is in a furor. There hasn't been any rioting yet, but the key word is *yet*. I think it's only because of the overwhelming police presence since the cross-burning. But if something isn't done soon, I don't think the peaceful protests will last. I'm positive they'll turn violent. It reminds me of situations I saw overseas. You can almost feel the trouble brewing."

"And what about your meet with those other cops?"

"It turned out pretty much as I expected. They are the scum of the earth. After ten minutes, I felt like taking a shower." Johnny opened a can of beer and said, "I really don't understand how people can be that way. It's unimaginable."

"Are you telling the captain who they are this time?"

He nodded. "I've got no choice. This was a special assignment, and I suspect they may know something about who did this cross burning; in fact, I wouldn't be surprised if they had something to do with it."

Michele looked concerned. "Johnny, are you serious? If you think that, you need to get out of this mess. You could be in danger."

Johnny laughed and held her face in his hands. "I know you're worried, but things don't work like that. When you're a cop, you do what needs to be done. Ordinarily, I would never dream of ratting on a fellow officer, but certain things demand a change in policy, and this is one of them. But don't worry. I'll be more than careful."

Michele snuggled up to him. "You better. You now have another little McCoy to look after, not to mention me."

Johnny leaned over and kissed her. "And how could I forget you, my sweet?"

Johnny called the captain that night, and they arranged to meet in the morning at the same Starbucks as before, and once again, they met at six-thirty. Both of them were on time, so they got their drinks and sat down, opting for an outside table and some privacy.

"Let's hear what you've got, McCoy. And please let it be something worthwhile."

"I don't know if it's worthwhile, and it's certainly not good. The officer I told you about before? I met with him and three others for beers. At the very least, they are racist assholes. And in my opinion, they shouldn't be on the force. Not anywhere. The kind of attitude they expressed is contagious in a bad way."

"So you think I should discipline them?"

"Captain, it's your call as to what to do, but at the very least, I'd have IA look into them. Don't mess me up though by doing something right away. Do that, and they'd know it was me."

The captain sipped his coffee and seemed to be giving it thought. "Okay, McCoy, but I need you on this full-time. I can't afford to waste a minute. As of next week, I'm officially assigning you to the task force, which means everyone will know what you're doing. It'll be out in the open."

"I can handle that, Captain, and I can even try to explain it by saying you're looking for long-range shooting expertise. Since I just won the competition, that won't be a stretch."

Helger nodded. "Good thinking, McCoy. I like that. Let's run with that explanation. I'll put it in motion today so that by Monday, it'll be done."

"Sounds good," Johnny said, and stood to go.

THE TASK FORCE

Johnny was working at the computer when his partner, Bruce, came up behind him and slapped his back. "So, you're not only a shooter but a rising star."

Johnny turned around and stared. "What are you talking about?"

"Didn't you see the promotions board? It's got several of the guys who made sergeant, one sergeant promoted to lieutenant, and good old Johnny McCoy, newly appointed to the serial-killer task force, not to mention the rank of detective."

Johnny acted surprised and jumped up, heading for the board. "What? No way. Let me see."

When he reached the board, he read through it and shook his head. "Son of a bitch. I'll take it. I didn't know you could make detective so quickly."

"Usually, you don't, but with what's going on with this serial killer, I guarantee you it had something to do with it. And I bet it comes with a pay bump too," Bruce said. "I know you can use that."

"That's no lie," Johnny said. "Michele has been hounding me about baby furniture for more than a week. Ever since we got the gender results."

"You son of a bitch," Bruce said. "You didn't tell me. Give it up. What's it gonna be?"

"A girl," Johnny said. "I was hoping for a boy, but Michele wanted a girl. I guess mamma got her wish."

"I wish you better luck than I had," Bruce said. "I had four girls before I had a boy."

"Damn," Johnny said. "I think I'd have given up long before number five. You must have wanted a boy pretty badly."

Bruce smiled. "I did. And we probably shouldn't have done it, but I'm glad we did. I love that little stinker."

"Well, I can't say what I'd do, but I was hoping for number two to be a boy so I could have stopped there. Now I'll have to think."

"I'd go for it," Bruce said. "Especially since your star is on the rise. And by the way, what are you going to be doing now that you're in with the upper echelon?"

Johnny laughed. "Hell, Bruce. I don't know. I just found out. I guess I'm gonna have to see the lieutenant or captain—or somebody."

Johnny waited in the hall outside the captain's office for almost twenty minutes. Finally, he came out and asked Johnny in. "Obviously, you saw the announcement," Helger said. "Anyone say anything?"

"No one out of the ordinary," Johnny said. "My partner, which is to be expected, and one other guy I know pretty well. Oh, and the lieutenant did too."

"All right," Helger said. "I think you should stay with what you're doing, and even act as if nothing's changed. But I want you to keep a close eye on everybody around you, and especially on those degenerates you mentioned."

"It won't be hard keeping an eye on them. They're always either up at the shooting range or over to Lily's sucking down some cold ones and talking trash."

"Then you need to insinuate yourself into their little group even more. Do what you have to, but do it. And remember, if we want to take action, we need hard evidence. Hearsay won't do it, and neither will the testimony from one other officer."

"Yes, sir. I'll do it." Johnny stood to leave, but stopped and turned around. "One more thing, sir. Is it possible to have access to the files? I'd like to see what's in there and if it might help."

The captain shook his head, and it looked as if he would say 'no,' but then he hesitated. "Let me think about it, McCoy. I have purposely controlled access, but I can see how it may be beneficial. Give me a day or so."

"No problem, Captain. I'll check back with you then."

Johnny made sure to stop at the range on his way home, and he was glad he did. As he suspected, Bobby was there, and so was Pete. They were shooting the Sako TRG-42, and using the .338 Lapua ammo. A lot of the more serious shooters were moving to the .338 Lapua because it outperformed the Winchester and most of the other ammo in long-range testing. Not to mention the Sako was now considered one of the best sniper rifles in the world.

Seeing them shoot the Sako made Johnny more suspicious than ever. It cost more to shoot a Sako, and the wait times to use it were longer. To top it off, he had to ask himself why a normal person would have to use the best sniper rifle. There were plenty of long-range rifles that would more than suffice.

Johnny approached just as they were winding up. "Hey, Bobby, Pete. What's up? Trying to get in some practice before next year's competition?"

"Only if you're not going to be in it," Pete said.

Bobby smiled and said, "Ain't that the truth."

"C'mon, Johnny. We're heading down to Lily's. Let's get a few mugs."

"I haven't even shot yet," Johnny said.

"Hell, you don't need to shoot. You're plenty good right now. C'mon. I'm buying the first round."

Johnny shook his head, then said, "Okay. Damnit, I always let you talk me into this."

"Something tells me that's on purpose," Bobby said.

Johnny pulled into Lily's parking lot right behind Bobby. Milt and Spence were just exiting their cars a few rows over. "Right on time," Pete hollered and waved.

They got a spot near the front window with two tables pulled together, and as promised, Bobby ordered the first round. "I'm paying for this one, but unless we get to round six, my card is closed," he said.

"Johnny, I heard you got promoted to the task force," Milt said. "And to detective, for Christ's sake. Nobody earns a badge that quick."

"Yeah, so I heard," Johnny said. "Actually, my partner told me this morning. I didn't even know. I guess this serial killer shit, breaks the rules."

"Are you shittin' me?" Pete asked. "They didn't tell you? You mean your partner had to tell you that they made you a detective?"

"Exactly," Johnny said. "The captain called me in after the shooting competition and asked if I'd be interested in joining the task force, and I shrugged and said, 'sure,' I wouldn't mind it at all. Next thing I knew, Bruce is patting me on the back and saying congratulations. I didn't know what for. For Christ's sake, I haven't even told my wife yet."

"That part doesn't interest me," Spence said. "But what are you planning to do now that you're on the task force?"

"That's easy," Johnny said. "I'm gonna find the motherfucker who's doing this. The hard part comes afterward."

"Meaning what?" Milt asked.

"Meaning, I'll have to decide whether to lock the fucker up or pin a medal on him."

Everyone laughed, and Bobby said, "You're an ass, Johnny."

They went two more rounds. One paid for by Pete and one by Spence. "You know what that means," Bobby said. "Next time, Johnny and Milt start the buying."

"Hell, yeah," the rest said, then they all gulped what was left in their mugs and walked out.

Johnny had a long ride home. In actuality, it was no longer than normal—it just seemed like it was. When he walked inside the apartment, he was once again greeted by the sweetest woman in the world. She kissed him softly, and Johnny said, "You don't know how much I needed that."

"Long day?" she asked.

"Long, yes, but both good and bad,"

"Tell me about the bad, so I can make you feel better, then you can tell me about the good, so you can make me feel better."

Johnny snuggled up to her and rubbed her belly while he snuggled. "I knew there was a reason why I loved you."

"And you're just now finding it? Shame on you, Johnny McCoy. I don't think you'll make much of a detective."

"How about if I take you in the bedroom, and we can figure out how your belly got so big."

Michele pursed her lips and looked to the ceiling. "Hmm, I might enjoy that. Let's go," she said, and grabbed his hand, leading him to the bedroom. About halfway there, she stopped, turned around, and said, "Oh, wait, we can't. Your daughter is in the other room."

ACCESS COMES WITH RULES

In the morning, Johnny found a note on his desk instructing him to call Margie.

"Margie, it's Johnny McCoy. You asked me to call?"

"The captain wants to see you ASAP," she said.

"Say no more," Johnny said. "I'm on my way."

"Anything new?" Helger asked as Johnny walked in.

He shook his head. "Same as always, so far. I had drinks with the four I told you about yesterday, and while they were still as disgusting as ever, there was nothing that pointed to evidence that might be used against them."

"Well, McCoy, I thought it over, and I'm going to grant you access to the files, but understand this comes with certain conditions."

"Such as?"

"Such as any access to the files has to go through Sahrina, who is the admin in that sector. You cannot even view the files without her knowing it. Is that understood?"

"Absolutely, Captain. And that's not a problem. I should only need access for a few moments at a time. It can all be done in her view."

"Good. If you can live with that, we're set. I'll call Sahrina and tell her you're okayed. She's on the third floor at the entry to the storage for Homicide."

"When are you planning on calling her because I would like to get to those files quickly?"

"I'll call her as soon as you leave, McCoy."

"In that case, I'm leaving, sir," Johnny said. "I'll see you when I have something to report."

"Don't make it long. I'm under a lot of pressure, as I'm sure you can guess."

Johnny visited Sahrina just after lunch. He presented his credentials, and she checked and verified he was approved for access to the files. She copied his ID and recorded it, then led him to the back row of cabinets where the files were kept. She removed the appropriate folders and steered him to a table he could use to look at them. "Don't leave here," she said. "When you're finished, call me and I'll get the files and return them, then I'll show you out. Those are the rules."

"Everybody has to go through this?" he asked.

"Everybody," she said. "Even the captain." Sahrina turned to walk away, but stopped. "Oh, and no photocopying or taking pictures. Understood? I will be checking."

"I got it," Johnny said.

He flipped through the file, slowly examining each page. Several of the accompanying pictures were gruesome and difficult to look at —especially the younger girls. He didn't fully understand the emotions involved, but it held true across the board, and it didn't matter if it was people or animals. Seeing a puppy hit by a car and killed drew a bigger emotional response than seeing an adult dog hit.

The report showed date and time the body was found, and the best estimate for the time the shooting occurred. The file contained a reference to a bullet retrieved from the body as well as a ballistics report, though that wasn't his forte and he didn't fully understand it. It also had an accompanying paper showing a map with a large red X to indicate where the body was found. The bullet itself was being kept in the evidence room, where all such items were kept.

In addition, there were sketches and more photos showing the scene, and where the body was in relation to items on the premises. There was a fingerprint report which looked pretty empty, but Johnny made a mental note to go through that later. And of particular importance was a trace evidence report, which he would go through in detail. For the time being though, he had to figure out how to get the file so he could study it at home.

He finally settled on snapping photos with his phone and then texting those photos to Michele. He then erased the photos and the texts so Sahrina wouldn't see in the event she really did check his phone when he left.

He read through the reports meticulously, though he couldn't make heads or tails of the coroner's detailed analysis. It contained too much medical jargon for him. Even as he thought that, he wondered who he knew that he might get to help him with understanding that.

As he continued to scan the files, he remembered a door he had seen near the back row of file cabinets. He glanced in all directions, then got up and casually walked that way, intent on finding out where it led.

It was located in an out of-the-way spot and not visible from the main part of the room. He approached the door slowly, then grasped the doorknob and tried to open it, but it was locked.

A young woman must have seen him and asked, "May I help you?"

Johnny said, "I'm trying to find the rest room. It's my first time here."

The young woman smiled and walked toward the rear. "Follow me, and I'll show you where it is. That other door goes nowhere. Or at least now it does. I think it used to be access to Personnel, but they closed it off long ago."

"No wonder it wouldn't open," Johnny said, and breathed a sigh of relief.

He remained in the restroom long enough to make it look good, then he exited and returned to examining the files. *If Sahrina knew I'd left them alone, she'd likely write me up.*

After another half hour, he carried the files back to Sahrina and handed them to her. "All finished," he said. "At least, for now."

"I'll need to see your phone," Sahrina said. "Sorry, but I do this for everyone."

Johnny handed her his phone. *Thank God I erased everything.*

Sahrina looked at the photos, the texts, and the emails, among a few other apps. "Okay," she said. "You're good to go."

"I'm glad to see such good security here. Does everyone go through this?"

"As I said, 'even the captain.' No exceptions."

"Glad to hear it," Johnny said, but it made him wonder how his Uncle Bob had gotten access if Sahrina had such a tight grip on it. *Unless that locked door to Personnel isn't always locked.*

I SAW THE FILES

Johnny called Margie first thing in the morning and asked about an appointment to see the captain. Within fifteen minutes, he called back.

"McCoy, I think we should do this after hours. How about tomorrow morning, usual place and time?"

"Got it, sir. See you then."

Johnny spent the day fighting fires (figuratively) in the Fourth District, and he did his best to calm tempers that were raging toward an out-of-control level.

"Hey, Maleeka," he said to a young black girl he knew from his patrols. "What are you doing out here? You know it's dangerous. You should be inside so you don't get hurt."

"Ain't worried 'bout bein' hurt, McCoy. I been playin' here all my life and nothin' has happened yet."

"I know, but that doesn't mean something won't happen. There's some nut loose who is shooting young girls—young black girls, so it's not safe for you to be running around in the open."

"I know. You told me yesterday. I didn't forget. I just didn't pay attention. I don't like staying inside. There's nothing to do, and besides, nobody's home."

"Your mom and dad working?"

"I ain't got no dad, and my mom is always working. She says she's gotta put food on the table. I don't know what she means by that 'cause I don't see much food. All I see is the junk she shoots in her arm."

Johnny's heart melted. His life had been bad enough, but he couldn't imagine what it was like for her. "Maleeka, how about if you come home with me. My wife will take care of you and feed you properly. We won't let you get hurt."

Maleeka stopped talking. Stopped moving even. She looked as if she were considering what Johnny proposed, then she shook her head and said, "McCoy, it's not that I don't trust you. I kinda do. But if there's one good piece of advice my rotten-ass mother gave, it was not to trust anyone especially if they were white. That's done me good so far, so I'm gonna stick with it. Thanks for your offer, but I'll just stay put."

All Johnny could do was nod. "Okay, Maleeka. If you change your mind, you let me know."

"I'll do that, McCoy, but don't count on it. I'll be fine." She turned and skipped down the street.

Johnny watched her go and prayed she'd be all right, then he went on his way, checking other parts of the district.

By the end of his shift, he'd advised four or five young girls to stay inside, and he felt pretty sure than none of them would listen to him. All he could do was hope they'd be all right.

He drove home that night saddened by his lack of effectiveness.

The only bright spot in his day happened when he got home and was greeted by the two best girls he knew—his wife and daughter. He sat on the couch and hugged them both and said, "Who's up for ice cream?"

"I am," Chloe screamed. "Can we bring Louise?"

"Honey, I don't think—"

"Of course, we can," Johnny said. "Give her a call."

Michele shook her head. "I wish just once, I'd have a vote in what goes on here."

"Someday, you might," Johnny said, "But not when ice cream is involved."

"Yeah, Mommy. Not with ice cream," Chloe yelled.

"Michele shook her head and smiled as she walked to the bedroom to change clothes."

Two hours later, Johnny and Michele returned from eating too much ice cream. They took Louise home and tucked Chloe in bed. She'd fallen asleep on the way home, as usual. And if experience was anything to go by, she'd be out for the night.

"Don't tell me it wasn't worth it," Johnny said to Michele as he came back to the living room. "We now have the rest of the night to ourselves."

"Uh huh," Michele said. "And I suppose next you're going to tell me that was your plan all along. That you didn't take her because you spoil her but because you wanted to spoil me."

"That's it exactly," Johnny said. "How did you guess?"

Michele laughed and kicked her feet up on the sofa. "You're incorrigible, you know that?"

"Whoa! You're going to have to stop using those big words on me. Remember, I'm just a former Marine."

"So Mr. Former Marine, how was your day? Anything exciting happen?"

"Kind of. It wasn't exciting, but it was sad."

"Tell me about it," Michele said.

Johnny told her about Maleeka and what she said. Michele seemed as heartbroken as he was. "Do you think it would do any good if I talked to her. Sometimes, women are trusted more, especially by other women."

"Would you do that? For real?"

"Of course, I would. I can't do it tomorrow because I go to the doctor's, but I can do it the next day. Why don't we plan on it?"

"Fantastic," Johnny said. "You can follow me into work, then leave when we're done. If you're successful, I'll bring her home."

"It's a deal," Michele said. "Now what about the captain and the task force?"

"I'm not sure. I'm meeting him tomorrow morning, so I'll be able to fill you in better afterward."

"Sounds good," Michele said. "Now, if you don't mind too much, I'm going to retire early. I'm beat."

"Go ahead," Johnny said. "I want to go through these files again to refresh my memory. Remember, I'm not supposed to have them, so I have to pretend I'm speaking from memory."

"Just make sure your *memory* isn't too good," Michele said. "Nobody will believe you if it is."

In the morning, Johnny got up and quietly sneaked out of the apartment so he didn't wake anyone. He had an early appointment with Helger.

Once again, Johnny met Helger at Starbucks, and once again, they sat outside and talked. "Anything, McCoy? I'm getting nervous. Every time we had cross burnings in the past, killings followed. I can't afford to have more killings. If we do, I think the east side will erupt."

Johnny nodded. "I might have to agree with you on that, Captain. It's a mess over there. Everybody is on edge, like they're waiting for something to happen."

"So you've got nothing?"

Johnny shook his head. "Nothing new," he said. "Though there might be *something*."

"What?"

"I looked through those files, and they didn't seem complete."

"What the hell does that mean?" Helger asked.

"I know I'm a new homicide detective, but I do know a decent amount about ballistics, and there didn't seem to be enough information in the file. If they had the bullet, and assuming it was from a long-range weapon, my guess is there should have been more information."

"And how would you handle this?"

"I'd like to take the bullet to my old sergeant and see what he can tell us. If that's not an option, I'd like to bring someone here to examine it. Captain, I don't know what's wrong, but *something* is. And we need to find out what."

"There's no way you can remove the bullet from the evidence room, but I might arrange it so you could get someone in to examine it. Would that do? Could this person do their work in the evidence room?"

"I don't know, Captain. I'd have to ask."

"Then get on it. Ask. But do it quickly."

Johnny put in a solid eight hours with his new partner, Denny, and though he looked for Maleeka, he didn't see her. Maybe she had taken Johnny's advice and stayed inside. *I hope she did.*

When Johnny got home that night, he told Michele he had to do special work for the captain, so he wouldn't be able to take her to see Maleeka. "We'll have to put it off for a day or so," Johnny said. "It's critical that I get this done."

"No problem," Michele said. "I can do it any day this week."

AN OLD FRIEND

Johnny got in early and told Denny he'd be working at the station all day. "I've got a lot of calls to make, buddy. I'm sorry about this."

"No problem," Denny said. "I know how it goes with you big shots."

Johnny dug through his contact list until he found the number he wanted. He sat back in the chair and dialed the phone.

"Camp Lejeune, Sergeant Blackwood speaking."

"I can't believe you're still there," Johnny said.

"Excuse me, sir. Who is this?"

"This is your former Marine, private, corporal, Johnny McCoy, sergeant."

"McCoy! You son of a bitch. What the hell are you doing? You close by. Want to meet up?"

"I wish I were, sergeant, but I'm in Cleveland. I'm a cop now."

"A cop? No shit? How'd it ever go with sniper school? I heard you graduated number two."

"Yeah, it went great. After school, I went overseas and shot a few people, then I came home, got married, then joined the force."

"Son of a bitch," Blackwood said. "Well, if you're not close by, you want something, so spit it out, and I'll see if I can help."

Johnny laughed. "You old dog. I always liked your get-to-the-point attitude. So let me tell you my problem. You may or may not have heard of our serial killer problem up here."

"I did. Goddamn sin is what it is."

"No shit about that," Johnny said. "But my problem is I think someone is fucking with our ballistics, but I don't know enough about it to swear to it. You know anyone who can help with that? If I recalled, you were pretty sharp in ballistics."

"Thanks, McCoy. I like to think I was, but I'm not even close to somebody you know better."

"What? Who?"

"Remember your old buddy, Moj?"

"Moj? What the hell does he have to do with it?"

"Everything," Blackwood said. "He's the head of the FBI's ballistics lab. Give him a call. Not only could help, I'm sure he'd be glad to hear from you. In fact, if you hang on, I'll get you his number."

Blackwood placed the call on hold while he looked up the number, then got back on. "Okay, McCoy, here it is: (212) 555-3297. That's his cell phone which, is probably easier to reach him on."

"Okay, sergeant. This has been a gold mine. I thank you immensely. And if it pays off, I'm gonna take you to dinner. Hell, I'll take all of us to dinner."

"Good luck," Blackwood said.

Johnny moved to a more private location to call Moj. He sat at the desk, kicked his feet up, and dialed. A moment later, he was connected.

"Hello?"

"Is this some asshole named Moj?"

Silence, then, "Judging by the fact that not many people know me by that name, and of those that do, even fewer are from the Cleveland area, I'm guessing that this is a dickwad known as McCoy."

Johnny laughed so hard he choked. "So they've taught you some deductive reasoning, I see."

"No, I've always had that, but since you recognized it, I'll assume that wherever the hell you are taught you what that means."

Johnny laughed even more. "Moj, how the hell are you?"

"Doing great," he said. "I assume Blackwood gave you my number."

"He did. Is that more of your deductive reasoning at work?"

"In fact, it is. But what's up? Why the call?"

"I'm with the Cleveland Police now, and we've got a major problem. And it's one that might be helped with some ballistics expertise."

"Ah, the serial killer?"

"You're familiar with it?"

"More than familiar. We offered to help several times, but on each occasion were politely turned down. But tell me what you've got and what your role is in it."

"As far as what we've got, I'm sure you know that. We've got a serial killer targeting African American women. And it's not the norm. He's killed and quit three or four times now. He just started up again last week."

"And your role?" Moj asked.

"Insignificant, but with an inside track. I have a personal interest in this. Remember my fiancé, who was black? She was killed by this guy."

"So you're in Homicide?"

"Just promoted, Moj. I was the department's rep in a long-range shooting competition, and I won for them. That gave me a solid in with the captain, who then assigned me to the task force as a detective. I'm calling you because something isn't right with the ballistics, and I'd love you to look at the reports."

"But I'm guessing you can't send the bullet to me. I'd have to come there."

"Exactly," Johnny said.

"Let me clear my calendar, Johnny, but I'm guessing I can get there the day after tomorrow. Just tell your captain that I don't want any bullshit. I want access, and I want cooperation. Understood?"

"Understood, Moj. But I must say, you're scaring me with that kind of talk. You sound like Blackwood."

Moj laughed with Johnny, then they both said goodbye and hung up.

IT'S BEEN A DAMN LONG TIME

Johnny waited at the airport exit for Moj. He almost missed him because he was expecting just Moj, but he had brought two others. He beeped the horn, then got out of the car and waved. "Over here, Moj."

After a long greeting and quick introductions to the others, they drove back to the station. "They keep a firm grip on these files, Moj. I don't know why, but we're going to be under scrutiny for sure."

Moj laughed. "Johnny, I'm under scrutiny every damn day. You don't know scrutiny until you've worked at the FBI. They assume everyone is a traitor, and every day you have to prove you're not."

Johnny turned toward the back seat. "Excuse me for not being inclusive in my conversation. It's been so long since I've seen Moj, I'm just trying to catch up."

Johnny noticed Amy laughing. "What's so funny?"

"You calling him Moj. I've never heard that."

Realization hit Johnny like a brick, and he was just then aware that he didn't know Moj's name. He'd always known him as Moj. Johnny shook his head. "Shit, Amy, I just realized—I don't know his name."

"It's Morris Oliver Johnson," DuMond said. "Moj for short. But I only know that because I knew him growing up."

"I'll be damned," Johnny said.

Twenty minutes later, they parked and went inside the CPD head-quarters and straight to Captain Helger's office.

"Captain, this is Morris Johnson, director of the FBI's forensics, and these are two of his experts, Amy and DuMond. They came here to see if they can help us on this case."

Helger reached out and shook hands with all of them. "Nice to meet you, and we're more than grateful for the assistance. As you might guess, this is more than a thorn in our side."

"First, to clear things up, Captain, it is *Assistant* Director Johnson, and I'm only in charge of the ballistics section of the forensics department. Forensics consists of many labs; ballistics is just one of them."

"Well, I'm guessing that's the one we need help with, so that's good. Now tell me what you need to get started."

Moj spoke up first. "Since I assume there is a chain-of-custody consideration, what needs to be done to allow us to take the bullets in question from the evidence lab to your forensics lab so my people can analyze them?"

Captain Helger nodded. "It requires a lot, including someone to meticulously document the entire process." He picked up the phone and dialed. "I'll put that in motion now."

He explained to whoever answered what he needed, then he hung up and got back to Johnny and Moj. "Done," he said. "They said they'd have it the bullets there within the hour."

"Sounds great," Moj said. "After that, we'll analyze them and my team will submit the results to you."

"All right, good. And thank you. We need all the help we can get on this."

Moj acknowledged his thanks, then we left Helger's office. "Might as well get some coffee," Johnny said. "It's going to be a while before they're ready."

About an hour later, Moj and his team followed Johnny to the CPD forensics lab, but they weren't greeted warmly. Everybody seemed to have a chip on their shoulder. Johnny noticed right away and spoke up.

"Hey, guys. Listen up. These are friends of mine from the FBI. They're here to help, not to piss people off. We've got a lunatic out there killing people, and all they are trying to do is find something —*anything*—that might help. They're not here to make anyone look bad. If you want to be pissed at someone, be pissed at me. I asked them to come."

What Johnny said seemed to lighten up the mood with some people—*some*. Others weren't convinced.

The lab supervisor approached wearing a smile. "Pay no mind to the assortment of sour faces. They'll get over it soon enough. Now tell me what I can do to help. Oh, and by the way, I'm Tasha. Tasha Brown."

Moj reached out his hand. "Morris Johnson," he said, "and these two geniuses are my experts on ballistics: DuMond Peters and Amy Cole.

Tasha nodded and said, "Follow me, and I'll get you set up so you can work undisturbed. I need to advise you though, you will have a shadow the whole time." She turned and gestured to a young woman standing beside her. "This is Cyndi Barstock, and she will be documenting everything for chain-of-custody. Unfortunately, it's necessary in today's times."

"Noted and understood," Moj said as he removed his jacket. "Let's get to work."

"Anything else you need?" Tasha asked.

Amy looked around, then said, "I don't see a comparison micro-scope. We'll definitely need one of those. Other than that, I think we're all right."

"I'll send it over right away," Tasha said. "And if you need anything else, call me."

THE RESULTS ARE IN

After two days—and almost two nights—Moj and his team seemed ready. We got together for an early morning meet at their hotel, and he presented his data.

"Before I start, let me say this should all be considered preliminary. More analysis needs to be done, but with that being said, it's a damn good starting point."

"Go on, Moj. I'm eager to hear."

"First, after carefully examining all the bullets, Amy determined they were definitely Lapua .338s. Not rare, but not seen that often, although lately their use has increased."

"What makes finding out they were Lapua .338s significant?"

"By itself, nothing. However, considering the circumstances, it says a lot. This ammo was developed, or conceived, by snipers for snipers. It may have been the first time ammo was developed for a specific purpose and then the rifles were made to accommodate it."

"I know a lot about the ammo, Moj. I *was* a sniper, remember? But what I'm interested in, is what does that tell us about the gun that fired it, if anything?"

Moj shook his head. "I'll let DuMond field that question."

"All it really does is limit the field—the suspect list, so to speak," DuMond said.

"Explain, please?" Johnny asked.

"The easiest way to explain it is using something else. It's like having a witness tell you they saw a black car leaving the scene of a crime, but they didn't know the make or model. With this it's not much different. You have a lot of guns that could have fired these rounds—a lot—but you have no idea which one it was, and there is no way of telling. We can match a bullet to a gun; that's no problem. But we need to have the gun first."

"How many guns are we talking about—gun types, I mean, not physical number."

DuMond shook his head. "I'd have to do more research to be sure, but at I can think of almost a dozen off the top of my head, and surely there's more than that."

"For grins, is the Sako TRG one of those guns?"

DuMond let out a noise that sounded like a snort. "Not only is it one of the guns, it is considered one of the top sniper rifles in the world. Why did you ask?"

"Because I saw a couple of racist assholes shooting them at a range."

"Must have been some wealthy patrons or a range that caters to them because the Sako TRGs cost a pretty penny."

"What's the price tag?" Johnny asked.

"I'm not positive, but probably four to five thousand. And that's just the start. The ammo is expensive as hell to shoot. A lot of shooters save money by doing reloads, but it's still costly."

"Okay, what else did you find?"

"The same gun definitely shot all the bullets," Amy said. "That's what the comparison microscope was for. We put two bullets, side by side, under the microscope and you can analyze them simultaneously. It left no doubt."

"One more thing," Moj said. "I don't even know what you can take from this, but a chemical analysis showed that the bullets—all of them—had been coated with HBN."

"What the hell is HBN?"

"The technical answer is it is Hexagonal Boron Nitride, but why it is used is a hotly debated issue. Some claim it to be the latest and greatest bullet-coating material. It is ultra-slippery, goes on clear (not powdery), and will not combine with moisture or potentially harm barrel steel. The cons are that the coating reduces pressure in the barrel, thereby reducing velocity."

"What's your take on it, Moj?" Johnny asked.

"Don't have a take. I haven't researched it enough to know. But I can tell you it messes with anything we might have gotten from knowing the velocity based on the gun that fired it—if we had that. Using coated ammo can affect velocity in too many ways."

"If it was coated with HBN, does that mean the shells were self-loaded?" Johnny asked.

"Probably," Moj said, "but not necessarily."

Johnny sat back and gave thought to what he'd heard. "So what does all this tell you?" he asked.

"It tells me two things: one is that you've got a serial killer with enough smarts (and money) to be using Lapua .338s, and secondly, something is foul in your department."

The second statement brought Johnny to an alert state. "What do you mean by that?"

"I mean, when we spoke to your forensics people, they were shocked to hear that little of this was included in the ballistics report because they had initially reported it."

"Are you serious?"

"More than serious, Johnny. We were skeptical because we read their reports and nothing was in there. When we told them that, they seemed legitimately surprised. Then one of the tech aides, walked to her computer and pulled up a copy of what was originally filed, and it had all of what we did, but what she had *was not* in the official report contained in the files."

"How the hell is that possible?" Johnny asked.

"Somebody had to change it," Amy said. "I can't think of another way."

Johnny looked over and saw Moj nodding. "I can't think of another way either," he said. "There's a rotten apple in CPD, and you've got to find him and find out why?"

"Son of a bitch," Johnny said. "This is hard to believe."

"Hard or not. The proof is there. The report we saw on that aide's computer was a real one, and it was a good one. It differed very little from our own. But it differed greatly from what was in the murder file."

"Would you mind coming to the captain's office with me so you can explain it?"

"Be happy to, but then we've got to be off. My boss called this morning about a pressing case."

"No problem," Johnny said. "It won't take long. Do you have a flight yet?"

Moj nodded. "Leaves at 3:40."

"Okay, that gives us plenty of time."

After reporting to Helger, who seemed as shocked as Johnny at the prospect of someone dirty in the department, Johnny drove Moj and his people to the airport. He got them there in plenty of time, walked them in as far as he could go, then headed back to his car, deciding to call it a day and drive home.

He wasn't five minutes away when a call came in from Denny, his partner.

"Hey, Denny, what's up? And don't give me any shit about ducking work. I've been putting in more hours than ever with these damn FBI agents."

"It's not that, Johnny, but you're not going to like it."

"What? Something wrong?"

"The killer struck again, and this time it was Maleeka."

"What? Shit. Motherfucker. I was supposed to get with her. Fuck, fuck, fuck. Where did it happen?"

"Not three blocks from her house. You know that little park the kids cross to get to the playground? It was right there."

"Son of a fucking bitch," Johnny said. "Son of a fucking bitch. This is on me, Denny. I was supposed to take Michele to try to convince

Maleeka to come home with us. I knew something like this would happen. I *knew* it."

"You can't blame yourself, Johnny. Just go home and rest. I'm sorry I called, but I didn't want you to hear it on the news without knowing. And sure as shit, it's going to be on the news."

NOW THAT WE KNOW, WHAT DO WE DO?

Johnny got home, and though he tried to be happy and optimistic, the news about Maleeka had devastated him. He kept trying to tell himself that now she was in a better place, but he didn't believe it. He never understood it when people said that. How the hell can dead be better than alive—no matter how bad alive is?

He shared his feelings with Michele, but not until Chloe had gone to bed. He sure as hell didn't want to taint her attitude toward life. Not as good as it was.

Michele was talking to him about the day when she stopped abruptly and turned toward the TV. "Oh, God, Johnny. There's been another one."

"I know. That's what I've been telling you. Maleeka was shot today."

"No," Michele said. "I mean another one since then. Look."

Johnny turned up the volume and paid close attention to the report.

"And yet another shooting tonight in Cleveland. And from the looks of the scene, it is definitely the work of the serial killer. Now known as 'The Cleanser' based on a letter he sent to the press. In the letter, published earlier, he accused the CPD of attempting to lure him out with their recent shooting competition. He also said if he had wanted to, he could have beaten the so-called champion, but he was not about to be lured into such an obvious trap. He also said he would continue to 'cleanse' the world of the filthy races until they were gone. And he signed the letter 'The Cleanser.'"

"Son of a bitch," Johnny said. "I can't believe it. Shit will hit the fan tomorrow. I better plan on getting in early."

Johnny reported straight to Captain Helger when he got in, and to his surprise, Helger was in. "This is a goddamn mess, McCoy. We've got to do something quickly."

"What do you know about this last killing, Captain?"

"I know the girl was found in the old abandoned subway tunnels, and she was strung up like a damn animal waiting to be skinned."

"The subway tunnels? How did anyone find her?"

"I don't think anyone actually found her. I think the pervert called it in to the press and told them where to look."

Johnny shook his head as if bewildered. "You mentioned she was strung up like an animal. Exactly how?"

"Like an animal, for Christ's sake. What difference does it make? And she's got more holes in her than a damn shooting target."

"Son of a bitch, Captain, you may have just hit on something."

"What? I didn't say anything."

"No, but you made me remember something. When I was a kid, my father would take me to the shooting range, but on the way there, he would usually stop to pick up reloads as well as targets."

"I imagine a lot of people do that," Helger said.

"I'm sure they do," Johnny said. "But I'd bet not many got targets like this. They featured black people strung up like you said, as if they were animals waiting to be skinned, and their hearts were highlighted so they stood out. The hearts were the bullseye."

"Good God," Helger said. "That's sick."

"And that's not all of it," Johnny said. "Remember the guys I told you about who were racist sons of bitches—the four cops?"

"What of them?"

"The leader of that group is the son of the man who sold the targets and reloaded the shells."

"Son of a bitch!"

"Even better, I saw him shooting a Sako TRG 42 at the range. That shoots the Lapua .338 ammo we found in the bodies, and it's known to be one of the best sniper rifles out there."

The captain reached for his phone and began dialing. "Chief, we need two warrants on the serial-killer case immediately. And don't have a piss fit, but one of them will be for a cop. In fact, if anything pans out, there will likely be three more for other cops."

Helger had the phone on speaker, so Johnny heard the chief when he responded. "I don't give a shit if the warrant is on the mayor. If they are a legitimate suspect, serve the damn thing. We need this over with. Now what are the details?"

"Hang on, chief. I'm going to let you talk to Detective McCoy. He can fill you in."

"Chief, what do you need."

"Damn, boy. You know what I need for a warrant. Names, addresses, everything and anything you're looking for. Why you suspect it's there. All of it."

"Let's do the names first. PJ Reynolds and his son Bobby Reynolds. I don't know if his legal name is Bobby or Robert. Same goes for his father. I've only ever known him as PJ. But Bobby works for the department, so I'm sure we have the proper information."

"Damn, McCoy, this better be good."

"I think it will be, sir."

"At PJ's house, we will be looking for any guns capable of shooting a Lapua .338 shell, as well as targets that depict black people strung up as if they were animals. We also need to search for Lapua .338 shells, especially reloaded ones, or ones that are coated with HBN."

"What the hell is HBN?" the chief asked.

"The technical people will know, sir. It's a special coating some shooters use."

"And what about the warrant for Bobby?"

"We're looking for the same Lapua .338 shells, but also a Sako TRG 42 sniper rifle. I saw him shooting it at the range, and I happen to know the range doesn't offer that gun for shooting, so I assume it belongs to Bobby."

The chief asked a lot more questions, mostly to cover his ass, then he said, "I'll get these right away. You tell Helger to get a team of people he can goddamn trust and be ready to go in twenty minutes."

"Yes, sir. We'll be ready."

Johnny hung up the phone and turned to Helger, who was just hanging up. "I've made the calls already. We'll have six officers ready to go in ten minutes. But, we will need SWAT as well," Johnny said. "I'll also contact the FBI." Johnny started to leave but looked back to Helger. "Do you know where to go?"

"I have it here somewhere," Helger said, and he shuffled papers on his desk while looking.

"Don't bother," Johnny said, and handed him a slip of paper with the addresses written down. "The top address is for PJ, the father, and the other is for Bobby. And if you don't mind a suggestion, sir. I'd send at least four officers to each address and do it simultaneously."

"You're right, McCoy. I'll make that call now. And get your ass down to see Lieutenant Gilbert. He'll be leading this operation, but I want you with him to give advice."

"Yes, sir," Johnny said and left the office, heading to see Gilbert.

SERVE THE WARRANTS

Johnny introduced himself to Lieutenant Gilbert, who seemed pleased to have him on the team. "I don't know where you've been for ten years, McCoy, but we could have used you.

"Sir?"

"Just joking with you, son. Helger said you're a good guy to have, and if what I saw at that shooting contest is any indication, he's right. So tell me what we've got. All I know are names and addresses."

Johnny filled Gilbert in on PJ and Bobby, as well as his knowledge of their racist views and previous activity. "I'm not saying there is concrete evidence at this point, Lieutenant, but there is enough smoke to take a closer look."

"We'll take a closer look, all right. I got one boy on the team who makes the IRS auditors look like pussies. And you know how those sons of bitches are—they'll crawl up your ass with a flashlight looking for shit."

The lieutenant looked at the time, then said, "Okay, McCoy, time to go. He then dialed someone on his cell and gave the same orders."

On the ride to serve the warrants, he called again. "Remember. Nobody goes in until you confirm with me. We want to do this simultaneously. For you Neanderthals, that means at the same time. Got that?"

After receiving acknowledgement, the lieutenant hung up. "Sometimes you have to talk like you don't like them, but I love them all. I'd be pissed if anything happened to any one of them."

Johnny smiled. "I understand, sir. I had DIs in the Marines like that."

Gilbert waited a few blocks away for his signal, and once it came, Johnny and Gilbert moved in with two other officers. At the same time, the other team of four officers moved in on PJ's house.

Johnny knocked on the door and served the warrant, but when he received resistance from Mrs. Reynolds, Gilbert burst through the door, handing her the papers as he did. "Warrant to search the premises, ma'am. Being an officer's wife, I'm sure you're familiar with the process."

"What's this for? You can't do this," she said.

"What it's for is all in the warrant, and yes, ma'am, we *can* do this. That's what a warrant is for."

"I'm calling my husband."

"I would suggest you do that, ma'am. I'm sure he will want to know."

Gilbert turned to Johnny and said, "You might want to call Helger and tell him to get warrants ready on the other three he mentioned, just in case."

"In case of what?"

"In case they're in on this with Reynolds and they catch wind of what went down here."

"Damn, Lieutenant, I didn't think of that. I'll call now."

After half an hour of searching, Bobby's truck screeched into the driveway, tires throwing dirt and gravel everywhere. He jumped out of the truck and raced to the house, where he was stopped by one of the officers.

"What the hell is going on here?" he asked. Then he pulled out a badge and showed it. "I'm a goddamn cop. I'm with Homicide."

At that point, he must have seen Johnny. "McCoy. McCoy, is that you? You rat motherfucker. You stinking cheese-eating bastard. What did you tell them?"

Lieutenant Gilbert walked in from the kitchen and got in front of Bobby. "Reynolds, this is my operation. The fact that I have McCoy with me has no bearing on this. If you want to address questions or concerns, do it to me. If you want to register complaints, do it to Captain Helger."

Bobby spat on the floor. "Helger, just what I thought. Him and that rat-shit motherfucker, McCoy are asshole buddies. I haven't done shit, and I'd like to see you prove otherwise."

"I'm sure if you've done nothing wrong, the search results will confirm that. Now have a seat and do not interfere."

"Got something here," an officer called from the basement. "Looks like a shitload of ammo to me, and it looks like what we're searching for."

"Bring it up and log it in, officer."

Gilbert stood next to Reynolds. "Lose some of that confidence, Reynolds?"

"Why should I lose confidence? It's my damn gun for God's sake."

"But are we going to find a match between that gun and the bullets that killed those girls?"

"What? Is *that* what this is about? You guys are nuts. I didn't shoot anybody."

"We'll see," Gilbert said. "In the meantime, I don't think you should try to go anywhere."

"Are you placing me under arrest, Lieutenant?"

"No. At least, not yet."

"Then I'll go anywhere I fucking want to go. How's that?"

"That's fine, Reynolds. Keep digging that grave. I'll be the one laughing in the end."

Gilbert called Helger from outside Bobby's house. "Sir, he's not cooperating, and I'm convinced he'll call his buddies before we leave the property."

"What the hell do you think we should do?"

"If you're asking, Captain, I'd execute the other warrants. I think McCoy told me they were on Spence, Pete, and Milt. I'd do it before Reynolds calls them and they ditch any evidence."

Captain Helger sighed. "All right, Gilbert. I can't say I disagree with you. I'd like to, but I don't. Stay there for fifteen more minutes to give the teams a chance to get to the other houses. Besides, they're still on the job right now."

"Wouldn't Bobby's partner have been alerted when he went home?"

"I thought the same, but I just checked, and he's still on the job."

"Okay," Gilbert said. "We'll hang out here for a few."

Ten minutes away, the second team served the warrant to PJ Reynolds, and he was about as cooperative as his son. "Fuck you and your fuckin' warrant," he said. "What the hell are you looking for?"

"A lot of things," Officer Jack Nance said. "Instead of me listing them, how about we just tell you when we find them?"

"Fuck you again."

"Damn," Jack said. "You've got some vocabulary there."

"Got the targets," an officer yelled from the basement.

"Bring 'em up," Nance said.

"All of them? There must be thousands."

"Bring 'em up. The more there are, the worse it will be for old PJ."

"Got shells here," another officer said as he walked inside. "Found them in a shed out back. Gotta be at least ten or twelve boxes—big boxes. And it looks like he's got stuff used to coat them. I recognize it."

"Is it HBN?"

"Don't know for sure. It's not in the original container, but I'd bet it is."

"Any guns?" Nance asked.

299

"Haven't seen any, but we've got a lot of looking yet to do. I think there's at least one more, if not two more sheds farther out back."

Nance nodded. "Take Burns and check them out. We're looking specifically for rifles that can shoot the Lapua .338 ammo."

"I'm familiar with it," Burns said. "If he's got any, I'll spot it."

Ten minutes later, the officers returned. Burns was carrying a rifle in one hand a two boxes of ammo in another. "This," he said while holding up the gun, "is a Sako TRG 42, the best sniper rifle in the world. And in my other hand are two boxes of Lapua .338s, and they appear to be coated."

"All right," Nance said. "I think we hit the jackpot. Now lock up, Mr. Pleasant, then search for any records of sales to other people, whether it's guns, ammo, or targets. I believe Mr. Reynolds just purchased a ticket to our friendly neighborhood jail."

Before leaving, the officers found enough paperwork to fill several boxes, which they loaded into the back along with the targets, ammo, and the gun.

"You need to piss or anything before we haul your ass out of here, Reynolds?"

"Fuck you."

"Is that a yes or no?"

"Fuck you twice."

"I'll take that as a *no*," Nance said.

IT FITS, BUT IT DOESN'T

Johnny and Gilbert waited on the test results from ballistics. Johnny felt a lot more comfortable with them now that Moj and his team had given them a heads up.

Gilbert walked in with two coffees and handed one to Johnny. "Come on, McCoy, it'll be a while before ballistics are in. Let's go up and see Helger."

Lieutenant Gilbert walked into the captain's office, followed by McCoy. "Gentlemen, any news?"

"We're waiting on ballistics, sir, but that probably won't get done until tomorrow."

"And we expect what from the results?" Helger asked.

"We don't know yet. If either of them is guilty, a match with their guns will show. If they are complicit, the shells might match. And if neither of those things happens, PJ's books might show us something."

"Like what?" Helger asked.

"Like who he's been selling shells and targets to. Let's face it, whoever is buying those targets is one sick son of a bitch. Whether he's the killer needs to be determined, but there's no question that he's sick."

While Gilbert and Johnny were sitting with Helger, Margie knocked on the door, then walked in and handed the captain a few papers. "These just came in, sir."

Helger scanned them quickly, then looked up to Johnny. "These are by no means complete, but an initial review of the books, show that both ammo and targets have been sold to Bobby Reynolds' partner and his other friends for the past two years. No matter how you look at it that doesn't bode well."

The captain dialed a number, then said, "Nance, get out to Bobby Reynolds' place and arrest him. I'm having them bring the others in as well."

Gilbert swallowed hard. "Sir, I know it's despicable, but I don't think you can arrest them for shooting at targets."

"I'll give them a choice, Gilbert. Leave the force voluntarily and get out of law enforcement, or be exposed to the public for what they are. If they choose the latter, I doubt they'd last two months before someone does them justice."

"I can't argue that, Captain."

"All right, listen up. It's been a long day, and I need to go home and rest. Let's pick this up in the morning when we should have results from ballistics, and hopefully more information from PJ's books."

"Sounds like a plan, Captain," Johnny said. "I'm beat myself."

Johnny went home and told Michele about his day, but only after Chloe was in bed.

"Dear, God," Michele said. "What horrible people."

"More than horrible," Johnny said. "I'm just glad the captain did something about it."

"Do you think they'll fight him on it?"

Johnny shook his head. "Not if they're smart. I think they'll thank any God they pray to for their luck and high-tail it out of the city before the captain makes it known what they are. Let me tell you, after what's happened in this city, their lives wouldn't be worth a dime if their racist views were known."

"Do you think this PJ guy might be the shooter?"

"No, not really. I do think, though, that he might very well know who the shooter is. Anyway, tomorrow will tell a lot. We'll get the ballistics results and we'll get the final analysis from PJ's books."

"Good luck," Michele said. "I just want this over with."

Johnny got in early and found a message to see Captain Helger. He gulped down a coffee, then headed upstairs. "He in, Margie?"

Margie nodded. "He's waiting."

"You wanted to see me, captain?"

"I did. The ballistics results are in, but you're not going to like them."

Johnny sat down. "No matches?"

Helger shook his head. "Nothing. The only thing we were able to confirm was that the coating—the HBN, or whatever—matches what was found on the bullets from the shootings."

Johnny perked up. "That's good, isn't it? Doesn't that tie PJ to the crimes?"

"Not really," Helger said. "All it does is tell us he coated the bullets of whoever did the shooting. At the best, it tells us that."

"So all we need to do is go through those books in detail and see who it might be. Who owns a gun that can shoot that ammo? Who buys that ammo?"

"I know you're getting excited, Johnny, but sit for a few minutes. I've already sent PJ's books to our financial forensics people. In fact, I've got the best person we have on it, and she's been on it since yesterday. Her name is Tess Green, and I'm expecting a report from her at any moment. So sit tight and relax."

"I hear what you're saying, sir. But it's tough after waiting so long to nail this son of a bitch. I just want it over with."

"I understand that, Johnny. Be patient a few minutes longer."

As we waited for information, Margie called and said Tess Green was on the line. The captain picked up. "Tess, I've got officer McCoy with me. I'm placing you on speaker so that he can hear."

"Captain, I—"

"No worries about Johnny. Just tell us what we need to know. Go ahead, Tess. You've got our attention."

"Remember, I told you about the sales of targets, ammo, and coated shells to a B&T Enterprises?"

"I do. And if I recall, you couldn't find them."

"We couldn't at first. We did Google searches and looked everywhere we could—except the logical places."

"Go on."

"Late last night, I looked into the database for the department of records, and lo-and-behold, there it was—B&T Enterprises."

"I assume there's more."

"There's a lot more, Captain, but I don't think you're going to like it."

"Like it or not, I need to know."

"B&T Enterprises is Bob and Trudy McCoy."

Johnny almost fell out of his chair. Even the captain was caught unaware. "You're sure about that?" Helgar asked.

"Absolutely, Captain. I'm looking at the entry from the department of records; in fact, when I compared signatures with what we have on record, it matched perfectly."

"Okay, Tess. Thanks. I'll call if I need anything else."

Helger leaned back and stared at Johnny. "I don't know what to say."

"I do," Johnny said. "I guess my father's whole family are racist bastards."

"This isn't proof of anything, mind you," Helger said.

"Nice try, Captain, but it's proof enough for me."

"I don't see how this could be. How could Bob do something like this?"

"Captain, now that I have this in front of me, it all makes sense. The first day I had access to the files, I noticed a door by the last row, where the files were kept. One of the admins told me it was a door to Personnel, but it had been locked for years. I'd bet anything that good old Uncle Bob has the key to that door. And I'd also bet he gets access to any other file with his personnel badge."

"You think he is the one who messed with the files?"

"I think there is no doubt. In fact, I think when we search his house—which we should do immediately—we'll find a rifle capable of shooting the Lapua .338s, and I'm further betting the lands and grooves will match."

"I hope you're wrong, Johnny."

"I hope so, Captain, but I don't think so."

IT RUNS IN THE FAMILY

"We've got plenty of time to do this today, Johnny. Do you want in on this? Or would you rather sit it out?"

"As much as it disgusts me, Captain, I wouldn't miss it for a million dollars. In a way, I feel responsible. I should have seen this coming."

"Nonsense. If anybody should have seen it coming, it was me, and I had no inkling. But if you're intent on going, do what you need to. I plan on getting this done within the hour."

"Yes, sir," Johnny said.

Johnny was sitting at his desk, pondering, when the call came to move. He jumped up, checked his holster, then exited to join the team. They made it to Bob's house within fifteen minutes, then knocked on the door and served the warrant, handing it to Trudy.

~

"What is this? Who—"

She must have looked and seen Johnny. "Johnny, what is going on? Why are they in my house?"

Johnny walked over to her. "It's a warrant, Aunt Trudy. They're searching for things Uncle Bob might have."

"Searching for what? What are they looking for? Goddamnit, somebody better tell me something." She stormed onto the porch, letting the screen door bang shut. "Bob, there are a bunch of cops here searching our house. And they have a damn warrant. And Johnny is here too. Yeah, our Johnny."

"All right, I'll be right there," Bob said. "Don't panic. And don't say anything."

Fifteen minutes later, Bob showed up. He pushed through the front door, flashed his badge, and yelled. "All right, what the hell is going on? I want answers, and I want them now."

Captain Helger walked in from the other room. "What do you need to know, Bob?"

The appearance of Helger must have thrown Bob. He gulped and lowered his voice. "Captain, what's going on? Why are all these people here?"

Captain never lost his composure. "The name B&T Enterprises mean anything to you, Bob?"

Bob seemed to give it thought, then shook his head. "No, can't say it does."

"No? B&T, as in Bob and Trudy? Doesn't ring a bell?"

"Come on, Captain. B&T could be anything. It could be Bill and Tom or Ben and Tony."

"You're right, Bob. It *could* be, but it's not. And do you know how I know that? It's because *your* signature is on record next to the name."

It looked as if Bob were going to respond when Nance called down from the attic. "Got a gun, Captain. And if I'm not mistaken, it's a Sako TRG. Got ammo too."

Captain Helger nodded to the officer standing next to him, and the man placed Bob in cuffs. "You want to confess now, Bob, or do you want us to drop you off in the Fourth with a sign on your back?"

Bob spat at the captain, then said, "Fuck you, Helger. I'm going to have your badge."

Helger wiped his face and looked at Johnny. "Don't you love it, Johnny? The good vocabulary always comes out on the guilty ones."

"Fuck you again."

"Based on your responses, Bob, I'm sure we're going to get a match from ballistics. After that, it won't be long before they put a needle in your arm. Unless, of course, the other prisoners get wind of what you're in for. In that case, I doubt you'd make it until then."

Helger led the way out, followed by Bob, Nance, and Johnny. The whole way, Bob shouted and screamed at Johnny.

"You traitorous son of a bitch. You cocksucker. You nigger-loving prick."

And the whole time, Johnny smiled but said nothing. His life was near complete. He had caught the asshole who killed Liz and all the other women, and he had upheld his honor while doing it. He was afraid he was going to have to put a bullet to someone's brain to resolve the matter, but this was far better. Besides, Bob wouldn't last long in prison. Especially not when they discovered he was the serial killer—which they would.

The sidewalks were crowded with reporters and flashing cameras, and voices shouting questions that all seemed to run together.

"Is he the killer?"

"Why did he do it?"

"Is this the Cleanser?"

Helger, being experienced at this, ignored them all with a brush of his hand. Johnny and Nance did their best, but they were still learning.

Suddenly, a woman bolted up the sidewalk, screaming the whole way. "Did you do this? You piece of shit. You've ruined my husband. You've ruined my life."

Johnny looked over and saw Bob's wife, Aunt Trudy. He stepped aside to stop her. "Aunt Trudy, don't make it worse. Calm down."

"Calm down? How can I calm down when you're putting Bob in prison? And all for killing a few niggers? Answer me that, Johnny."

She screamed that, then she pulled out a gun and shot Johnny. She shot three times, and all three shots hit his chest. He staggered, then recovered and reached for her, then she shot again. The last one did him in, and he fell to the sidewalk.

By the time he hit the ground, several officers subdued her and took away her gun. Other officers knelt to give aid to Johnny, while another called the ambulance.

THE NEWS ISN'T GOOD

Michele got a call from Captain Helger, a surprise enough, but the content was worse.

"Mrs. McCoy, I'm afraid there's been a terrible development. Johnny was shot."

"What? How? When? Is he all right?"

"We don't know yet, Mrs. McCoy. He was sent away in the ambulance. I've got a car on the way to pick you up now. So please remain as calm as possible. They'll be at your house momentarily."

Michele paced the floor, continually looking out the window for the patrol car. While she waited, she called the sitter and explained the situation. "Please pick up Chloe from school, but don't tell her what happened. I'll do that when I get home."

The patrol car arrived, and twenty minutes later, they were at the Metro hospital, a Level 1 Trauma Center on West 25th in Cleveland.

Michele rushed to the ER, but as she entered the room, a doctor met her, shaking his head. "If you're Mrs. McCoy, he didn't make it."

She fell backward, but was caught by Nance, who had been waiting for the results. "Easy, Mrs. McCoy. Please take it easy. Think of the baby."

The doctor told Nance to set her in a nearby chair, then he examined her. "I think it's just shock," he said, "which is understandable. Is there anyone who could stay with her for a night or two?"

Helger walked in just then. "Somebody get hold of Dom Camino. He raised Johnny like a father. I'm sure he or his wife could help out."

Clorinda showed up within fifteen minutes, and Dom showed up soon after. He had tears running down his cheeks. "Not like that boy didn't go through enough. His mother, his fiancé, now this. God bless his soul. And he was a good kid too. Never a mean thought, even after all he went through."

Clorinda stayed with Michele for the next several days, doting on her and granting her every wish. And she kept Chloe home from school and kept the TV off so she didn't know what was going on.

The day of the funeral reporters were there from all across the United States camped out in front of St. Roccos Church.

The news of Johhny's death made headlines across the country, mostly due to the gruesome nature of the crimes.

Hero Cop Catches Cleveland Serial Killer

It was estimated there were over four thousand police cars, some with four officers inside each car. Law Enforcement Agencies from as far away as Canada came. The FBI and Secret Service sent members as well. The procession traveled from I-90 and looked like a Blue Sea train.

The procession was led by CPD's Motorcycle Unit and CPD's helicopter maintained air presence over the procession. The U.S. Marine Core's Honor Guard stood at attention next to the hearse as Johhny's casket was loaded.

As the funeral procession left the church, thousands of Cleveland residents stood holding signs

Thank You, Johnny We Love you, Johnny.

The day of the funeral, Michele told Chloe what had happened. Chloe cried for hours on end. She couldn't stop. Her father had been her life, just as she was his.

"Why is Daddy gone? Why can't he come back?"

"At the funeral, Michele tried her best to comfort Chloe, but she couldn't. She could barely comfort herself."

The only comfort came from two very different sources. The first was when a long line of fellow officers walked solemnly to the coffin. One by one, they placed their CPD badges on top of the coffin, then blessed themselves and said a prayer—some silent, some aloud.

But as much a surprise as that was, the bigger surprise came from a completely unexpected source. The line of officers was about halfway finished, when crowds of black people showed and walked through the cemetery gate. They then placed flowers and wreaths next to Johnny's grave. Some of them knelt in front of his coffin and prayed. Others just blessed themselves and said a silent prayer. By the end of the service, thousands had come, and on the way home, thousands more lined the streets, their car lights turned on in acknowledgement of Johnny.

He was a hero, though he never intended on being one. He was a hero because of what he'd done.

At the cemetery, CPD's Honor Guard Unit as well as the Marines Fired a 21-Gun Salute. Michele was presented with a folded American Flag by the Cleveland police chief and another one from from the Marines.

"Are all those people here for Daddy?" Chloe asked.

Michele hugged her. "They are, dear. Your daddy was a great man."

ACKNOWLEDGMENTS

This book is dedicated to the men and women of law enforcement.

I wish to thank the Cleveland Homicide Department as well as Detective James Gannalo (NYPD Retired) for help and advice on ballistics.

ABOUT THE AUTHOR

 Charles Jason Smith of Cleveland, Ohio, was a police officer who served 15 years. He served the last 7 years of his career, as a tactical sergeant of a Warrant Fugitive Task Force. Charles was severely injured during an incident where an armed suspect took his own baby hostage. He earned many commendations and was highly decorated.

Following the end of his law enforcement career he built a successful real estate business and became a nationally recognized expert. In 2003, Charles wrote a book "From Cop to CEO" which sold over 500,000 copies. Charles then sold his business and began writing fiction. To date, he has written another book, one screenplay and one TV Pilot.

www.goldbadgeproductions.com

americanhomicidedetective.com